Intermediate Education Board for Ireland

Intermediate Education Board for Ireland report, 1894

Intermediate Education Board for Ireland

Intermediate Education Board for Ireland report, 1894

ISBN/EAN: 9783742810472

Manufactured in Europe, USA, Canada, Australia, Japa

Cover: Foto ©Andreas Hilbeck / pixelio.de

Manufactured and distributed by brebook publishing software
(www.brebook.com)

Intermediate Education Board for Ireland

Intermediate Education Board for Ireland report, 1894

CONTENTS.

	PAGE
REPORT,	iii
APPENDICES,	3

I. List of persons of whom a sufficient number will be selected, with the approval of the Lord Lieutenant, to conduct the Examinations in 1894 (Rule 6), . . . 3

II. List of Examiners selected, with the approval of the Lord Lieutenant, to conduct the Examinations in 1884, . 9

III. Extracts from the Reports of the Examiners, 1894, . 11

Greek,	11
Latin,	17
English,	25
Prize Writing,	37
French,	38
German,	45
Italian,	46
Spanish,	47
Celtic,	48
Domestic Economy,	48
Elementary Mechanics,	50
Plane Trigonometry,	50
Algebra and Arithmetic,	51
Euclid,	51
Algebra,	54
Arithmetic,	58
Book-keeping and Accounts,	58
Natural Philosophy,	58
Chemistry,	60
Drawing,	60
Shorthand,	64
Music,	65
Botany,	67

IV. Lists of Schools to the Managers of which Results Fees were paid in 1894, and amounts of such Fees, . 68

V. The Burke Memorial Prizes, ... 68

REPORT

OF THE

INTERMEDIATE EDUCATION BOARD

FOR IRELAND

FOR THE YEAR 1894.

TO HIS EXCELLENCY, ROBERT, BARON HOUGHTON,
K.P., P.C.,

LORD LIEUTENANT GENERAL AND GENERAL GOVERNOR OF IRELAND.

MAY IT PLEASE YOUR EXCELLENCY,

We, the Commissioners of Intermediate Education (Ireland), submit to your Excellency this our Fifteenth Report.

The number of students who gave notice of their intention to present for examination in 1894 was:—

Boys.	Girls.	Total.
6,279	2,067	8,346

being an increase of 549, or 9·0 per cent, in the case of boys, and an increase of 211, or 11·4 per cent, in the case of girls, and a *total* increase of 10 per cent. on the corresponding numbers in 1893, and a *total* increase of 81·7 per cent. on the corresponding numbers in 1892.

In the nine previous years the numbers were :—

—	Boys.	Girls.	Total.
1885	4,504	1,215	5,719
1886	4,681	1,848	6,029
1887	5,012	1,460	6,472
1888	4,903	1,636	6,549
1889	5,281	1,578	7,159
1890	4,541	1,682	5,763
1891	4,196	1,444	5,627
1892	4,714	1,622	6,866
1893	5,780	1,556	7,596

See Table I.

The number of students who presented themselves for examination in 1894 was :—

Boys.	Girls.	Total.
5,816	1,855	7,623

In the nine previous years the numbers were :—

—	Boys.	Girls.	Total.
1885, . .	4,128	1,556	5,151
1886, . .	4,848	1,199	5,542
1887, . .	4,015	1,815	5,251
1888, . .	4,551	1,507	6,048
1889, . .	4,548	1,525	6,588
1890, . .	5,948	1,763	5,236
1891, . .	8,856	1,500	5,154
1892, . .	4,294	1,465	5,759
1894, . .	5,365	1,706	6,874

The examinations, which commenced on 12th June and extended over eleven days, were held at 226 centres, in 68 different localities, as follows:—

BOYS

Localities	No. of Centres	Localities	No. of Centres
Armagh,	1	Kilrush,	1
Atherry,	1	Kingstown,	2
Athlone,	2	Letterkenny,	1
Athy,	1	Limerick,	4
Ballymena,	1	Lisburn,	1
Ballymoney,	1	Lismore,	1
Bangor,	1	Listowel,	1
Belfast,	11	Londonderry,	4
Blackrock,	3	Langford,	1
Bray,	1	Lurgan,	1
Cahersiveen,	1	Mallow,	2
Callan,	1	Midleton,	2
Carlow,	2	Monaghan,	2
Carrick-on-Suir,	1	Mountrath,	1
Cashel,	3	Mullingar,	1
Castleknock,	3	Multyfarnham,	3
Cavan,	1	Navan,	1
Charleville,	1	Nenagh,	3
Clongowes Wood College,	3	New Ross,	1
Clonmel,	1	Newry,	2
Closkeagh,	1	Omagh,	1
Coleraine,	2	Farranstown,	1
Cookstown,	3	Queenstown,	1
Cork,	11	Santry,	1
Dingle,	1	Skibbereen,	1
Doon,	1	Sligo,	2
Drogheda,	1	Strabane,	1
Dublin,	28	Tipperary,	1
Dundalk,	3	Thurles,	1
Dungannon,	2	Tipperary,	3
Dungarvan,	1	Tralee,	1
Ennis,	3	Tuam,	1
Enniscorthy,	1	Waterford,	4
Enniskillen,	1	Westport,	1
Fermoy,	2	Wexford,	1
Galway,	2	Youghal,	1
Holywood (Down),	1		
Kilkenny,	3		
Killarney,	3	Total,	162

B

GIRLS.

Localities.	No. of Centres.	Localities.	No. of Centres.
Armagh,	1	Killarney,	1
Athy,	1	Letterkenny,	1
Balbriggan,	1	Limerick,	1
Ballymena,	1	Londonderry,	4
Ballymoney,	1	Longford,	1
Belfast,	0	Monaghan,	1
Bray,	1	Mountmellick,	1
Carrickmacross,	1	Mullingar,	1
Celbridge,	1	Navan,	1
Cookstown,	1	Newry,	1
Cork,	4	Omagh,	1
Dalkey,	1	Portadown,	1
Dublin,	14	Rathfarnham,	1
Dundalk,	1	Sligo,	1
Dungannon,	1	Tralee,	1
Enniscorthy,	1	Waterford,	3
Gorey,	1	Wexford,	1
Holywood (Down),	1		
Kilkenny,	1	Total,	64

The following Table shows the distribution of Centres between the Four Provinces :—

—	Leinster.	Ulster.	Munster.	Connaught.	Totals.
Boys,	63	34	35	10	142
Girls,	28	26	9	1	64
Total,	91	60	44	11	226

One hundred and sixty-six gentleman and sixty-four ladies were employed as Centre Superintendents, being an average of one Superintendent to every 35 boys and 29 girls examined, respectively.

The number of students who passed the Examinations was :—

Boys.	Girls.	Total.
3,419	1,104	4,573

In the nine previous years the numbers were :—

—	Boys.	Girls.	Total.
1885,	2,436	735	3,171
1886,	2,685	825	3,510
1887,	2,636	959	3,595
1888,	2,872	1,222	4,094
1889,	2,844	1,174	4,018
1890,	2,333	767	3,100
1891,	2,304	774	3,078
1892,	2,589	734	3,323
1893,	2,041	955	3,296

The proportion *per cent.* of those examined who passed was :—

Boys.	Girls.	Boys and Girls.
55·6	50·2	53·0

The proportions in the nine previous years were as follows :—

—	Boys.	Girls.	Boys and Girls.
1885,	49·	49·4	61·3
1886,	61·6	63·5	65·6
1887,	56·9	79·5	60·
1888,	63·1	61·1	57·6
1889,	58·7	68·2	61·3
1890,	59·1	40·3	50·9
1891,	50·7	49·3	50·0
1892,	50·1	53·5	57·7
1893,	57·7	55·9	57·3

Exclusive of over-age students the proportion per cent. of those examined who passed was :—

Boys.	Girls.	Boys and Girls.
60·8	59·0	60·2

Exclusive of over-age students the proportions in the three preceding years were as follows:—

—	Boys.	Girls.	Boys and Girls.
1891, .	59·7	59·0	59·6
1892, .	59·4	58·5	57·4
1893, .	60·6	57·2	59·

The number of students to whom were awarded £50 Prizes (Senior Grade), and Exhibitions (Rules 21–26) was :—

Boys, 324 ; Girls, 105 ; Total, 429.

The number of students to whom were awarded prizes in books was—

Boys, 358 ; Girls, 101 ; Total, 459.

The number of students to whom were awarded Prizes for Composition under Rule 35 was :—

Boys, 123 ; Girls, 67 ; Total, 190.

The number of students to whom were awarded Commercial Prizes under Rule 32 was :—

Boys, 16 ; Girls, none.

The amount of Results Fees paid to Managers of Schools on account of the Examinations in 1894 was:—

Boys, £35,104 4s. 9d.; Girls, £10,674 18s. 3d.; Total, £45,779 3s. 0d.

Of the students, 4,523, who passed the Examination, Results Fees were paid on 4,212, being an average Fee of £10 17s. 4½d. per student.

The following Table shows the distribution of Results Fees between the Four Provinces, and the number of Schools in each Province, to the Managers of which Results Fees were paid:—

Provinces.	Amount of Results Fees paid.		Total.	No. of Schools.		Total.
	Boys.	Girls.		Boys.	Girls.	
	£ s. d.	£ s. d.	£ s. d.			
Leinster, . . .	18,463 4 8	4,069 0 0	17,543 4 0	61	47	108
Ulster, . . .	8,633 1 0	5,083 0 0	13,781 3 0	55	53	108
Munster, . . .	11,800 9 0	1,208 10 0	12,877 0 0	55	17	72
Connaught, . . .	1,617 9 0	213 10 5	1,831 0 0	15	3	18
Gross Total, . .	35,104 4 0	10,674 10 5	45,779 0 0	166	120	306

The values of the Burke Memorial Prizes awarded in 1894 were :— *See Table XI, and App. V.*

Boys—
First Prize, £14 16s. 0d.
Second Prize, £9 5s. 0d.

Girls—
Prize, £9 5s. 0d.

FINANCE.

Our Balance Sheet for the year 1894, in respect of the original Endowment (Table X. *infra*), shows a surplus of £1,971 11s. 6d. (including a sum of £1,015 12s. 6d., Income Tax to be refunded by the Commissioners of Inland Revenue).

From this surplus must be deducted a sum of £1,236 13s., being the proceeds of securities sold (for payment of Results Fees and current expenditure pending refund of Income Tax), leaving a net surplus for the year of £734 18s. 6d., subject to liabilities estimated at about £200.

Our expenditure therefore in respect of the original Endowment in the year was almost equal to our present annual income from that Endowment.

The Local Taxation Account (see Table IX.) shows that the Receipts under the Local Taxation (Customs and Excise) Act, and as interest on Securities, amounted to £47,008 16s. 9d., and that the expenditure from that Account on Results Fees and Exhibitions for 1894 was £43,527 9s. 3d., as against £27,956 7s. 8d. expended out of same Account in the previous year, 1893, £18,538 15s. 1d. in 1892, and £5,097 2s. 8d. in 1891.

The increase in this expenditure from 1891 to 1893 has been £22,857 13s. 3d., and from 1893 to 1894 there has been a further increase of £15,571 2s. Our anticipations, therefore, of increased expenditure, as stated in our Reports for the years 1892 and 1893, have been realised.   And as the causes which have led to this progressive increase are still in operation, we have to count upon a still further expenditure in 1895 and again in 1896, which will, in all probability, more than exhaust the entire of the then annual income.

It will thus be seen that the time is fast approaching to which we were obliged to look forward in the framing of our Regulations for the expenditure of the new Fund, and at which, but for the amount held in reserve during the first few years of the working of the new system, it would not be possible to meet the expenditure under the Scheme.

As regards this amount temporarily held in reserve it must be observed that any Regulations which would have exhausted the entire Local Taxation Income in one of the early years would necessarily have required, in each succeeding year, a sum far in excess of the income of the year before. In other words, an expenditure necessarily progressive for a series of years could not be borne by a yearly income substantially invariable in amount, if the expenditure were so framed as to exhaust the Fund in the first year of the working of the system.

It is further to be observed that even in 1894, taking the state of both Accounts into consideration, our total expenditure has exceeded what can safely be calculated on as our permanent income from all sources after the year 1896, in which year the last payment will be made under the guarantee of the Treasury of interest at 3½ per cent on our original endowment of £1,000,000.

EDUCATION.

Notwithstanding the fact that the conditions of passing the examination generally were somewhat more stringent in the case of Boys than in 1893, the percentage of those examined who passed rose from 57·7 per cent. to 58·8 per cent. In the case of Girls there was a still further advance, viz., from 53·9 per cent. to 59·2 per cent. of those examined.

The favour with which the Preparatory Grade is regarded is shown by a further increase in the numbers presenting themselves for examination, this being in the case of Boys from 1,778 to 2,120, and in the case of Girls from 492 to 525. In this Grade

the percentage of passes in the case of Boys was very nearly equal
to that in 1893, being 62·2 compared with 62·4. In the case
of Girls the percentage fell from 50·3 to 51·2. The percentage,
however, in 1892 of Girls who passed was only 47·8.

With regard to the Commercial side of our examinations, there
was a very considerable increase in the number of students who
qualified for special Commercial Certificates, which were awarded
under the same conditions as in 1893, 78 students (76 Boys and
2 Girls) having so qualified, compared with 27 students (Boys)
in 1893; and the number of special Commercial Prizes gained
rose from six in 1893 to sixteen in 1894. In addition, however,
to these students, many others, as in 1893, who did not aim at
obtaining Commercial Certificates, availed themselves of the
opportunity of presenting themselves for examination in certain
Commercial subjects.

For the second time Shorthand (Pitman's System) formed a
subject of examination. The number of Boys presenting themselves in this subject fell from 618 in 1893 to 403 in 1894; the
percentage of passes increased from 42·7 to 60·4.

The number of Girls who presented themselves fell from 43
to 33, and the answering was scarcely as good as in 1893.

Detailed information respecting the answering of the students,
Boys and Girls, in the different subjects will be found in the
Extracts from the Reports of the Examiners (Appendix V.)*

TABLE I.—Showing the Number of Students who presented themselves for Examination in the years 1885, 1886, 1887, 1888, 1889,
1890, 1891, 1892, 1893, and 1894.

—	PREPARATORY GRADE.									
	1885.	1886.	1887.	1888.	1889.	1890.	1891.	1892.	1893.	1894.
Boys	—	—	—	—	—	—	—	1,488	1,778	2,129
Girls	—	—	—	—	—	—	—	301	487	425
Total	—	—	—	—	—	—	—	1,889	2,265	2,554

* Copies of Extracts from the Reports of the Examiners were transmitted to all
Managers of Schools in Ireland to whom Results Fees were paid in 1894.

TABLE I.—Showing the Number of Students who presented
1888, 1889, 1890, 1891, 1892,

	JUNIOR GRADE.									
—	1885.	1886.	1887.	1888.	1889.	1890.	1891.	1892.	1893.	1894.
Boys—of the prescribed age,	3,230	3,414	3,627	4,163	3,812	3,076	3,064	3,177	2,467	3,449
Do., Over-age,	75	103	81	109	101	64	107	—	240	283
Total	3,305	3,517	3,708	3,714	3,078	3,134	3,171	3,177	2,687	3,732
Girls—of the prescribed age,	755	899	954	1,153	1,307	923	941	785	715	861
Do., Over-age,	18	14	6	19	17	18	39	—	50	61
Total	773	893	973	1,113	1,244	903	966	735	627	879
Gross Total	3,840	4,680	4,540	4,577	4,317	4,997	4,135	3,942	3,534	3,482

	SENIOR GRADE.									
—	1885.	1886.	1887.	1888.	1889.	1890.	1891.	1892.	1893.	1894.
Boys—of the prescribed age,	735	944	230	944	274	810	774	195	960	719
Do., Over-age,	9	2	18	7	19	13	6	7	40	43
Total	725	248	353	361	704	826	725	925	846	862
Girls—of the prescribed age,	74	99	80	109	101	109	94	95	82	90
Do., Over-age,	9	—	1	3	4	1	7	1	6	9
Total	77	99	80	112	105	110	66	95	92	169
Gross Total	819	949	830	835	839	935	934	937	843	844

themselves for Examination in the years 1885, 1886, 1887, 1893, and 1894—*continued.*

MIDDLE GRADE.										
1885.	1886.	1887.	1888.	1889.	1890.	1891.	1892.	1893.	1894.	
564	547	575	542	547	534	459	412	568	504	Boys—of the prescribed age.
28	79	83	17	84	16	34	–	75	180	Do. Over-age.
592	676	612	569	591	549	457	412	578	754	Total.
318	197	159	271	265	279	241	227	361	259	Girls—of the prescribed age.
18	18	16	9	19	6	9	–	94	58	Do. Over-age.
998	211	969	980	616	787	669	727	969	867	Total.
580	788	672	698	897	730	707	718	944	972	Gross Total.

TOTAL.										
1885.	1886.	1887.	1888.	1889.	1890.	1891.	1892.	1893.	1894.	
4,213	4,705	4,448	4,407	4,446	4,609	6,791	4,507	4,825	5,172	Boys—of the prescribed age.
113	180	167	149	144	135	185	7	389	616	Do. Over-age.
4,328	4,543	4,513	4,551	4,859	5,943	5,855	4,904	5,388	5,815	Total.
1,978	1,173	1,999	1,488	1,043	1,371	1,373	1,404	1,610	1,766	Girls—of the prescribed age.
88	94	18	74	83	89	94	1	91	119	Do. Over-age.
1,948	3,199	1,919	1,577	1,888	1,909	1,809	1,405	1,700	1,886	Total.
5,791	4,149	5,993	6,948	6,539	5,795	6,164	6,709	6,874	7,829	Gross Total.

TABLE II.—Showing the Days and Hours at which Examinations in the several subjects of the Programme were held in 1864.

Date	Preparatory Grade		Junior Grade		Middle Grade		Senior Grade	
	Subject	Hours	Subject	Hours	Subject	Hours	Subject	Hours
Tuesday, 13th June.	Latin, (Classical.)	10-1 1-4	Latin, (Classical.)	10-1 1-4	Latin, (Classical.)	10-1 1-4	Latin, (Classical.)	10-1 1-4
Wednesday, 14th June.	English, (Journal.)	10-1 1-4	English, (Journal.)	10-1 1-4	English, (Journal.)	10-1 1-4	English, (Journal.)	10-1 1-4
Thursday, 15th June.	Algebra, (Journal.) Arithmetic,	10-1 1-4	Algebra, (Journal.) Arithmetic,	10-1 1-4	Algebra, (Journal.) Arithmetic,	10-1 1-4	Algebra and Arithmetic, (Journal.) Plane Trigonometry,	10-1 1-4
Friday, 16th June.	History, Euclid, (Journal.) French,	10-1 10 1-2 4	Drawing, Practical Geometry, (Journal.) Euclid, (Journal.) Euclid, (Journal.)	10-11.30 11.30 11 11.30-1 30 1-30 5	Drawing, Practical Geometry, (Journal.) Euclid, (Journal.) Euclid,	10-11.30 11.30-12 12-1.30 1-30	Drawing, Perspective, and Properties of Solids, Sections, and Shadows, Euclid, (Journal.) Euclid,	10-11 30 11.30-1 30 1.30-4 1-4
Saturday, 17th June.	French,	10-1	French, (Journal.) Natural Philosophy,	10-1 1-4	French, (Journal.) Natural Philosophy,	10-1 1-4	French, (Journal.) Natural Philosophy,	10-1 1-4

(continued)

BOYS.

TABLE V.—Showing the number of Students to whom £50 Prizes (Senior Grade), and Exhibitions were awarded.

—	Senior Grade, £50.	Middle Grade, £30 a year, tenable for two years.	Junior Grade, £20 a year, tenable for three years.	Preparatory Grade, £15 tenable for one year.	Total.
Boys, . . .	17	40	161	153	321
Girls, . . .	8	15	53	27	105
Gross Total, .	25	55	180	159	429

TABLE VI.—Showing the number of Students to whom Prizes in Books were awarded.

—	First Class Prizes.	Second Class Prizes.	Third Class Prizes.	Total.
Boys:—				
Preparatory Grade,* . .	—	—	140	140
Junior „ . . .	29	41	49	119
Middle „ . . .	10	11	32	53
Senior „ . . .	0	8	25	40
Total, . . .	51	61	246	352
Girls:—				
Preparatory Grade,* . .	—	—	20	20
Junior „ . . .	11	71	33	63
Middle „ . . .	5	6	14	25
Senior „ . . .	8	6	0	23
Total, . . .	24	33	75	131
Gross Total, . .	75	93	321	459

* £2 Book Prizes, only, were awardable in the Preparatory Grade

TABLE VII.—Showing the number of Students to whom Prizes in Composition were awarded. (Rule 85).

—	Greek.	Latin.	English.	French.	German.	Italian.	Celtic.	Spanish.	Total.
BOYS:—									
Preparatory Grade, £3, .	5	6	8	6	3	—	6	—	62
Junior „ £2, .	4	10	11	5	4	—	5	—	89
Middle „ £3, .	6	5	4	4	3	5	2	1	23
Senior „ £4, .	6	5	4	2	1	2	4	—	22
Total . .	20	25	27	17	11	5	17	1	120
GIRLS:—									
Preparatory Grade, £2, .	—	5	6	—	4	—	1	—	16
Junior „ £2,	—	5	5	6	6	—	—	—	22
Middle „ £3, .	1	6	5	2	6	1	—	—	19
Senior „ £4, .	—	1	5	5	4	—	—	—	18
Total, . .	1	10	21	14	19	1	1	—	67
Gross Total, .	21	35	48	51	30	6	18	1	190

TABLE VIII.—Showing the number of Students to whom Special Commercial Prizes were awarded. (Rule 82.)

—	Number.	Value.
BOYS:—		£
Junior, £10, ...	3	30
Do., £7, ...	4	28
Do., £5, ...	5	25
Middle, £6, ...	3	15
Do., £3, ...	3	6
Total, . . .	16	94

TABLE IX.—ACCOUNTS of the BOARD (Land Taxation (Scotland and Ireland) Act) for the year ended 31st December, 1894.

(A) INVESTMENT ACCOUNT.

	Securities		Cash				Securities		Cash	
	£ s. d.		£ s. d.				£ s. d.		£ s. d.	
Balance at 1st January, 1894,	10,333 4 10		—		Balance on 31st December, 1894,		10,333 4 10		—	

(B) INCOME ACCOUNT.

	£ s. d.			£ s. d.	
Balance on 1st January, 1894,	100 0 0		Remittances,	3,000 10 0	
Sum of Land Taxation Duties, 1893–1894,	42,000 0 0		Sundry Fees,	40,000 10 0	
Income of Annuities,	2,300 0 0		„ on account of the Fees LIFE,	200 0 0	
„ on Cash on Deposit,	200 0 0		Balance on 31st December, 1894,	1,171 0 0	
Sundry Fees refunded 1893,	20 10 0				

TABLE X—ACCOUNTS of the BOARD (original

(A) CAPITAL

	Securities.			Cash.		
	£	s.	d.	£	s.	d.
Balance on 1st January, 1894,	1,021,501	17	0	6,476	16	3
Surplus Income from Revenue Account,						
Securities purchased, viz.—Government 2¾ per cent. Stock,	6,447	19	0	1,226	13	0
Cash proceeds of Securities sold,						
	£ 1,028,041	16	0	7,656	9	3

(B) INCOME

Expenditure.				£	s.	d.	£	s.	d.
In respect of the year 1893:—									
Cash Balance as per Report of 1893, ... £5,919 19 1									
Results Fees for 1893 to be refunded, ... 1 10 3				5,921	9	4			
Income Tax refunded,				560	4	5			
Results Fees refunded, 1893,				4	0	0			
Legislative Expenses refunded,				9	3	1	6,755	16	10
[Cr. Balance, 1893, £6,451 16s. 8d.]									
In respect of the year 1894:—									
Interest on Securities,				33,187	15	0			
" on Cash on deposit,				189	11	10			
Examination Fees,				1,817	7	1			
Do. (late) Fees,				6	12	4			
Sale of Waste Paper,				2	1	1			
Restitution,				1	4	0			
Petty Expenses refunded,				0	0	6			
Sale of Publications,				2	2	11	36,366	0	0
Cash proceeds of Securities sold,							1,226	13	0
[Cr. Balance, 1894, £958 19s. 0d.]									
							£ 44,348	10	1

* The net liability against this Balance is estimated at £958

Endowment) for the year ended 31st December, 1894.

ACCOUNT.

	Securities.			Cash.		
	£	s.	d.	£	s.	d.
Cash invested in Government Securities (as per Contra),	—			6,422	16	3
Securities sold,	1,260	6	0	1,280	13	0
Balance on 31st December, 1894,	1,034,681	10	0	—		
£	1,386,941	16	0	7,408	9	3

ACCOUNT.

PAYMENTS.		£	s.	d.	£	s.	d.
In respect of the year 1893:—							
Administration—							
Incidentals,		41	7	10			
Printing and Stationery,		14	16	4			
Cost of Audit, 1893,		100	0	0			
					156	3	0
Examinations—							
Printing and Stationery,		68	12	4			
Petty Expenses,		15	10	6			
					84	2	3
Results Fees,		—			7	10	10
Minor Prizes,		—			82	0	0
In respect of the year 1894:—							
Administration—							
Permanent Salaries,		2,962	5	0			
Writers,		499	4	0			
Rent,		96	19	0			
Printing and Stationery,		89	0	0			
Incidentals,		393	13	0			
Building addition to Offices,		346	10	0			
Architect's Fees,		41	7	0			
					4,372	18	7
Examinations—							
Examiners' Remuneration,		5,398	0	0			
Do. Locomotive Expenses,		54	17	0			
Do. Incidental and Petty Expenses,		9	0	0			
Clerks Superintendents' Remuneration,		3,161	0	0			
Do. Locomotive Expenses,		459	0	0			
Do. Incidental and Petty Expenses,		587	3	0			
Hire of Rooms,		343	0	0			
Printing and Stationery,		1,446	0	0			
Petty Expenses,		704	0	0			
Locomotive &c.,		14	11	7			
					11,696	9	2
Rewards—							
Money Prizes and Exhibitions, 1894 (new Awards),		3,851	0	0			
Balance Exhibitions of 1893 and 1892,		3,707	10	0			
Results Fees,		10,850	3	0			
Medals and Minor Prizes,		981	1	0			
					17,389	14	0
Miscellaneous—							
Income Tax to be refunded,		—			1,018	12	0
On account of Surplus Income (transferred to Capital Account),		—			6,422	16	3
Balance,		—			368	19	0
					£42,299	19	7

* All Expenses of Administration and Examinations are paid out of the original Endowment of the Board, payments from the Local Taxation Grant being limited for Results, Fees and rewards to Students.

TABLE XI.—THE "NURSE MEMORIAL FUND."

Account for the Year ended 31st December, 1894.

CAPITAL ACCOUNT.

Government 2½ per cent. Consols, £3,226 16s. 1d. | Balance on Dec. 31, 1894, . £1,226 16s. 1d.

Income Account.

	£	s.	d.			£	s.	d.
Balance on 1st January, 1894, ...		1	0	11	Prizes (vide page 11), ...	33	8	0
5 Jan., Quarter's Dividend on 2½ per cent. Consols,		8	1	3	Printing and Stationery, ...	0	12	6
5 April, „ „ „ „ „		8	1	3	Balance on Dec. 31, 1894, ...	0	16	1
5 July, „ „ „ „ „		8	1	3				
5 Oct., „ „ „ „ „		8	1	9				
	£34	16	7			£34	16	7

Given under our Common Seal
　　this 15th day of March, 1895.

(L.S.)

Present at Board Meeting when Seal was affixed,

T. J. BELLINGHAM BRADY,　}
JOHN C. MALET,　　　　　 } *Assistant Commissioners.*

NAMES OF THE COMMISSIONERS

OF

INTERMEDIATE EDUCATION (IRELAND).

Right Hon. J. T. BALL, LL.D., D.C.L., Chairman.
Right Hon. C. PALLES, LL.D., Lord Chief Baron of the Exchequer
　　in Ireland, Vice-Chairman.
Rev. GEORGE SALMON, D.D., D.C.L., LL.D., F.R.S., Provost, Trinity
　　College, Dublin.
The Right Hon. O'CONOR DON, D.L., LL.D.
Rev. W. TODD MARTIN, D.D., D.LIT.
DAVID G. BARKLEY, Esq., LL.D.
His Grace The Most Rev. WILLIAM J. WALSH, D.D., Archbishop
　　of Dublin.

ASSISTANT COMMISSIONERS.

T. J. BELLINGHAM BRADY, LL.D.
JOHN C. MALET, M.A., F.R.S.

APPENDIX I.

LIST of PERSONS from whom the Examiners for 1894 were
selected with the approval of the LORD LIEUTENANT
(Rule 5).

GREEK AND LATIN.

Armour, Rev. James B., M.A. (R.U.I.)
Barrott, Rev. R.
Beare, John I., M.A., F.T.C.D.
Bryce, A. Hamilton, LL.D.
Bury, John B., M.A. (Dub.), F.T.C.D.
Butler, Rev. M. J., B.A., D.D.
Coxan, Arthur, M.A. (R.U.I.), B.A. (Dub.), Sen. Mod., T.C.D.
Cutler, W. E. P., B.A., 1st Sen. Mod., T.C.D.
Crowe, Rev. Jeremiah, St. Patrick's College, Thurles.
Dickie, John, B.A. (Dub.), 1st Sen. Mod., T.C.D.
Dongan, T. W., M.A., Ex-Fellow, St. John's College, Cambridge,
    Professor of Latin, Queen's College, Belfast.
Dowdall, Rev. Launcelot D., LL.B. (Dub.), M.A. (Oxon.), 1st Sen. Mod.,
    T.C.D., University Student.
Doyle, Charles F., M.A. (F.R.U.I.), B.A. (Dub.), Sen. Mod., T.C.D.
Doyle, Robert, M.A. (Dub.), Moderator, T.C.D.
Hamilton, A. B., B.A., LL.B. (R.U.I.)
Hayes, Rev. Lawrence J., D.D., Professor, St. Patrick's College, Thurles.
Healy, John, B.A.
Hitchcock, Francis R. M., B.A., Dub., 1st Sen. Mod., Univ. Student, T.C.D.
Keane, Charles, M.A. (Dub.), Sen. Mod., T.C.D.
Kelly, Very Rev. J. J., Canon.
Keris, R. C. M., B.A., 1st Class Classical Honours, London.
Maguire, Rev. R., Professor of Classics, St. Patrick's College, Maynooth.
Mannix, Rev. D., Professor, St. Patrick's College, Maynooth.
M'Glone, Rev. Peter, D.D.
M'Neill, Hugh A., B.A., R.U.I.
M'Rory, Rev. Joseph, D.D., Professor, St. Patrick's College, Maynooth.
Molahan, John P., M.A. (Dub.), Sen. Mod., T.C.D.
Montgomery, Robert, M.A., University Student (R.U.I.), B.A., 1st Class
    Classical Tripos, Cantab.
Montgomery, Malcolm, M.A. (Dub.), 1st Sen. Mod., T.C.D., Univ. Student.
Morgan, Rev. W. Moore, M.A., T.C.D.
Newsome, Clarence, M.A. (R.U.I.), Sen. Mod., T.C.D.
O'Farrell, Very Rev. J., Canon.
O'Neill, Rev. James.
Palmer, Arthur, M.A. (Dub.), F.T.C.D., Prof. of Latin, Univ. of Dublin.
Patton, Rev. Samuel, M.A.
Purser, Louis C., D.LITT., F.T.C.D.
Rea, Rev. James, B.D. (Dub.), Sen. Mod., T.C.D.
Ridgeway, William, M.A. (Dub.), Professor of Greek, Queen's College,
    Cork; Fellow, Gonville and Caius College, Disney Professor of
    Archaeology, Cambridge.
Rowan, William H., M.A., Univ. Student (R.U.I.)
Roberts, Theodore M., M.A. (Dub.)
Rutherford, H. E., B.A., LL.B.

Ryan, Rev. Innocent, Professor, St. Patrick's College, Thurles.
Sandford, Philip George, M.A. (Dub.), Professor of Latin, Queen's College, Galway.
Starkie, W. J. M., M.A., F.T.C.D.
Thompson, D'Arcy W., M.A. (Cantab.), F.R.U.L, Professor of Greek, Queen's College, Galway.
Tyrrell, Robert Y., M.A., D.LITT. (Dub.), F.T.C.D., Professor of Greek, University of Dublin.
Wilkins, Rev. George, M.A. (Dub.), F.T.C.D.
Wilson, Herbert, B.A. (Dub.), 1st Sen. Mod., T.C.D.

ENGLISH.

Allen, Henry J., M.A. (Dub.), 1st Sen. Mod., T.C.D.
Bailey, William F., M.A. (Dub.), 1st Sen. Mod., T.C.D.
Barry, Rev. Louis Aug., LL.D. (Dub.), 1st Sen. Mod., T.C.D.
Bastable, C. F., B.A., (Dub.), Prof. of Political Economy, Univ. of Dublin.
Boyd, Andrew, M.A. (R.U.L)
Brown, Samuel Lombard, B.A. (R.U.I.)
Carmichael, Rev. Frederick F., LL.D. (Dub.)
Cherry, Richard R., M.A., LL.D. (Dub.), Reid Professor of Constitutional and Criminal Law, T.C.D.
Clancy, Rev. John J., Professor of English Literature, St. Patrick's College, Maynooth.
Coghlan, Rev. Daniel, St. Patrick's College, Maynooth.
Colclough, John D.
Cooke, John, M.A. (Dub.), Professor, Church of Ireland Training College, Kildare-place.
Coyne, William P., M.A. (R.U.I.)
Craig, D., M.A. (R.U.I.), Professor of English Literature, Catholic Training College, Drumcondra.
Cusack, John.
Dixon, G. Y., M.A., F.C.S.
Dixon, W. M., B.A., LL.B., 1st Sen. Mod., T.C.D.
Donnellan, Rev. James, St. Patrick's College, Maynooth.
Donovan, R., M.A. (R.U.I.)
Evans, Rev. Henry, D.D.
Fahmatnhaugh, Godfrey, B.A. (Dub.), 1st Sen. Mod., T.C.D., Univ. Student.
Fitzgibbon, Henry M., M.A. (Dub.), Senior Mod., T.C.D.
Fitz-Henry, William A., M.A., LL.B.
Fogarty, Rev. M., St. Patrick's College, Maynooth.
Gilliland, W. L., B.A., LL.B. (Dub.), Senior Mod., T.C.D.
Graham, Wm., M.A. (Dub.), Professor of Jurisprudence and Political Economy, Queen's College, Belfast.
Hardy, William J., LL.D. (Dub.), Sen. Mod., T.C.D.
Harrison, Thomas, B.A., LL.D. (R.U.I.)
Henry, Rev. J. Edgar, M.A. (R.U.I.)
Herdman, John O., M.A., Sen. Mod., T.C.D.
Humphreys, John, B.A.
Hyde, Douglas, LL.D.
Joyce, P. W., LL.D., Ex-Professor, Board of National Education.
Keane, A. H., B.A.
Kehoe, Daniel, B.A. (Dub.), Senior Mod., T.C.D.
Lennox, P. J., B.A. (R.U.I.)
Lyster, Mary A., M.A.
Lyster, Thomas W., B.A. (Dub.), 1st Senior Mod., T.C.D., Assistant Librarian, National Library of Ireland.

M'Bride, Rev. J. B., B.A. (R.U.I.)
M'Donald, Rev. Walter, St. Patrick's College, Maynooth.
Magennis, William, M.A. (F.R.U.I.)
MacMullen, S. J., M.A. (R.U.I.), Professor of History and English Literature, Queen's College, Belfast.
Maoran, Henry S., M.A., F.T.C.D.
Murphy, James.
Nash, Rev. Francis L., M.A. (Oxon.)
Newcombe, Rev. J. D. E., B.A., B.D. (Dub.), Sen. Mod., T.C.D.
Nicolls, Archibald J., LL.B. (Dub.)
O'Leary, Rev. Patrick, St. Patrick's College, Maynooth.
O'Loan, Rev. Daniel, St. Patrick's College, Maynooth.
Osborne, R. E., M.A.
Owens, Rev. R., St. Patrick's College, Maynooth.
Park, John, M.A. D.LITT. (R.U.I.), F.R.U.I., Professor of Logic and Metaphysics, Queen's College, Belfast.
Rea, Rev. George T., M.A.
Redmond, Frederick, B.A. (Dub.), Sen. Mod., T.C.D.
Rolleston, T. W., B.A., T.C.D.
Rowley, James, M.A., Professor of Modern History and English Literature, Univ. College, Bristol.
Savage-Armstrong, George F., M.A. (Dub.), F.R.U.I.; Professor of History and English Literature, Queen's College, Cork.
Scratton, Thomas, B.A. (Oxon.)
Semple, R. J., M.A.
Smyth, Rev. J. Paterson, B.A., LL.B. (Dub.), Sen. Mod., T.C.D.
Stanton, Lacy Vere.
Steele, L. Edward, B.A. (Dub.), Professor in the Church of Ireland Training College, Kildare-place.
Story, Mary, M.A., University Student, R.U.I.
Taylor, John F., B.A.
Welland, Rev. Charles W., B.A. (Dub.), Sen. Mod., T.C.D.
Whelan, Rev. Denis, St. John's College, Waterford.
Whitty, R. G. J., M.A. (Dub.), Sen. Mod., T.C.D.
Wilhan, Rev. Thomas B., M.A. (Dub.), 1st Sen. Mod., T.C.D.
Witherow, Rev. J. M., M.A. (R.U.I.)
Wright, A. E., B.A. (Dub.), 1st Senior Mod., T.C.D.

FRENCH.

Amours, F. J., B. ès L. French Master, Glasgow Academy.
Barbier, Paul E. H., Lecturer, French Language and Literature, Univ. Coll., South Wales, Cardiff.
Barbier, Georges H., Lecturer in French, The Athenaeum, Glasgow.
Barrère, A., Prof. of French, Royal Military Academy, Woolwich.
Boïelle, James, B.A. (Paris).
Bué, Henry, B. ès L. (Univ. Gall.)
Cogery, A., B.A., L.L. (Paris), Examiner in French, Trinity Coll., London.
D'Auquier, Rev. E. C., M.A. (Cantab.)
D'Auquier, T. C.
Dupuis, Alexandre L., D.A.
Egerton, Charles W., M.A. (Dub.), Senior Mod., T.C.D.
Hogan, Rev. J. F., St. Patrick's Coll., Maynooth.
Jaman, Elphege, Assistant Examiner in the University of London.
Ludwig, A., B.A. (Univ. Gallia).
M'Weeney, Edmond J., M.A., M.B. (R.U.I.)

Maas, J. F. P.
Migot, N., B. es L.
Nül, Otto C., M.A., London.
Nolan, Pierce L., B.A.
Oger, V., French Lecturer, Univ. Coll., Liverpool.
Spencer, Frederic, M.A., PH.D., Professor of Modern Languages, University College, Bangor.
Voegelin, A., B.A. (London).

GERMAN.

Boweringe, Rev. H., St. Patrick's College, Maynooth.
Buchheim, C. A., PH.D., Prof. of German in King's College, London.
Fischer, E. L.
Hager, Herman, PH.D.
Heinemann, F., Prof. of German, Crystal Palace School of Arts & Sciences.
Hennig, Curt, M.A.
Lange, Franz, PH.D., Prof. of German, Royal Mil. Academy, Woolwich.
Meissner, A. L., PH.D., Prof. Modern Languages, Queen's Coll., Belfast.
Oswald, E., M.A., PH.D. (Goettingen), Instructor in German to the Royal Naval College, Greenwich.
Schlomka, C., M.A., PH.D.
Seim, Albert M., M.A., LL.B. (Dub.), Sen. Mod., L.O.D., PH.D., Professor of German, University of Dublin.
Steinberger, Valentine, M.A. (R.U.I.), Professor of Modern Languages, Queen's College, Galway.

ITALIAN.

Farinelli, A., B.A., Professor of Italian, University College, London.
Morosini, Francesco.
O'Keeffe, Rev. Barth. A., D.D.
Ricci, Luigi, Prof. City of London College.

SPANISH.

Steinberger, Valentine, M.A., R.U.I., Professor of Modern Languages, Queen's College, Galway.

CELTIC.

Connolly, William P., B.A.
Flannery, T.
Hogan, Rev. Edmund, S.J.
McCarthy, Rev. B., D.D.
Molloy, John, B. es L.
Murphy, Rev. James E. H., M.A. (Dub.).
O'Duffy, Richard J., Hon. Sec., Society for the Preservation of the Irish Language.
O'Growney, Rev. Eugene, Professor, St. Patrick's College, Maynooth.
Olden, Rev. Thomas, B.A.

MATHEMATICS.

Alexander, J. J., M.A., (R.U.I.), B.A. (Cantab.)
Allman, George J., M.A., LL.D., F.R.S., Ex-Professor of Mathematics, Queen's College, Galway.
Anglin, A. H., M.A. (R.U.I.), B.A. (Cantab.), F.R.A.S., Professor of Mathematics, Queen's College, Cork.
Bergin, William, M.A. (Dub.), Sen. Mod., T.C.D.
Bernard, Rev. J. H., M.A., B.D. (Dub.), F.T.C.D.
Browne, J. J.
Burnside, Wm. S., M.A. D.SC. (Dub.), F.T.C.D., Prof. of Mathematics, Univ. of Dublin.
Carroll, Rev. P. J.

Coates, W. M., M.A. (Dub.), B.A. (Cantab.), Sen. Mod., T.C.D., Fellow of Queen's College, Cambridge.
Culverwell, Edward P., M.A., F.T.C.D.
Dawson, H. C., B.A. (Dub.), 1st Sen. Mod., T.C.D., M.A. (Cantab.), Fellow of Christ's College, Cambridge.
Dickey, Rev. R. H. F., M.A., B.D.
England, John, M.A. (Dub.), Professor of Natural Philosophy, Queen's College, Cork.
Fry, M. W. Joseph, M.A. (Dub.), F.T.C.D.
Graham, Christopher, M.A. (Dub. and Cantab.), 1st Sen. Mod., T.C.D., Ex-Fellow, Gonville and Caius College, Cambridge.
Griffin, Gerald.
Griffin, Robert W., LL.D. (Dub.)
Hughes, Rev. William, D.D. (Dub.)
Inwood, Thos. W., B.A., Professor of Mathematics, St. Gregory's College, Downside, Bath.
Johnston, J. P., M.A. (Dub.), Sen. Mod., T.C.D.
Johnston, Swift P., M.A. (Dub.), 1st Sen. Mod., T.C.D., Univ. Student.
Joly, C. J., M.A., 1st Sen. Mod., University Student, T.C.D.
Kelly, Patrick.
Larmor, Joseph, M.A. (R.U.I.), M.A. (Cantab.), Senior Wrangler, Fellow of St. John's College, Cambridge, F.R.S.
Leebody, John R., D.Sc. (R.U.I.), Professor of Mathematics and Natural Philosophy, Magee College, Londonderry.
Lennan, Rev. Francis, D.D., Professor of Mathematics and Natural Philosophy, St. Patrick's College, Maynooth.
Lyster, Arthur R., B.A. (Dub.), Sen. Mod., T.C.D., Assistant Astronomer, Dunsink Observatory.
M'Weeney, Henry C., M.A. (R.U.I.), Sen. Mod. (T.C.D.)
Minchin, George M., M.A. (Dub.), Professor of Applied Mathematics, Royal Indian Engineering College, Cooper's Hill.
Moran, Rev. Francis, M.A. (Dub.)
O'Dea, Rev. Thomas, Professor, St. Patrick's College, Maynooth.
Orr, Wm. M'F., M.A. (R.U.I.), Sen. Wrangler, Fellow of St. John's College, Cambridge; Prof. of Applied Mathematics and Mechanism, Royal College of Science, Ireland.
O'Sullivan, A. C., M.A. (Dub.), F.T.C.D.
Panton, Arthur W., M.A., D.Sc. (Dub.), F.T.C.D.
Power, Rev. Thos. R., Prof. of Mathematics, St. Patrick's Coll., Thurles.
Rambaut, Arthur A., M.A., D.Sc., Astronomer Royal of Ireland.
Rea, James C., B.A. (R.U.I.), Professor in the Church of Ireland Training College, Kildare-place.
Roberts, W. R. Westropp, M.A. (Dub.), F.T.C.D.
Russell, R., M.A. (Dub.), F.T.C.D.
Smith, Charles, M.A. (R.U.I.), 1st Sen. Mod. (T.C.D.), Univ. Student.
Tarleton, Francis A., LL.D. (Dub.), F.T.C.D.
Warren, Rev. Isaac, M.A.
Yates, James, B.A., Sen. Mod., T.C.D.

ARITHMETIC AND BOOK-KEEPING.

Dowd, Rev. James, B.A. (Dub.), Sen. Mod., T.C.D.
Bond, H. S., Royal Bank of Ireland.
Dowling, E. Hughes, Math. Tutor, University College, Stephen's-green, Dublin.
Dowling, P. A. E., B.A.
Ellis, Wm. E., M.A., LL.B. (Dub.), Local Gov. Auditor, Ireland.
Farrelly, Daniel.

Fitzpatrick, S., Prof. of Mathematics, Catholic Training Coll., Drumcondra.
Irwin, Rev. Charles K., D.D., (Dub.)
Keoghan, Rev. Patrick, B.A. (R.U.I.)
Macbeth, Rev. John, LL.D. (Dub.)
O'Brien, Edward T., Accountant, Mining Co. of Ireland.
Sutcliffe, Rev. Thomas, B.A. (Dub.)
Tristram, Rev. John W., M.A. (Dub.), Sen. Mod., T.C.D., Diocesan Inspector and Secretary, Diocesan Board of Education.
Warnock, Rev. W. J., B.A. (R.U.I.)
Whitton, Frederick A., Accountant, Representative Church Body.

NATURAL PHILOSOPHY.

Anderson, Alexander, M.A., Fellow of Sydney Sussex College, Cambridge, Professor of Nat. Phil., Queen's College, Galway.
Barrett, W. F., F.R.S.E., Professor of Physics, R.C.Sc.I.
Brown, Wm., Demonstrator in Physics, Royal Coll. of Science, Dublin.
Coffey, George, B.E. (Dub.), Sen. Mod., T.C.D.
Doherty, J. J., LL.D. (Dub.), Sen. Mod., T.C.D.
Fitzgerald, George F., M.A. (Dub.), F.R.S., F.T.C.D.
Johnston, Margaret K., M.A.
Joly, John, D.Sc., F.R.S.
Larmor, Alex., M.A. (R.U.I.), B.A. (Cantab.), Fellow of Clare College, Cambridge.
Moore, Hugh Kaye, B.A. (Dub.), 1st Sen. Mod., T.C.D.
Oram, John E., M.E. (R.U.I.), M.A., Ex-Professor of Mathematics, &c., Univ. of Windsor, N.S.
Preston, Thomas, M.A. (Dub.), F.R.U.I., Sen. Mod., T.C.D.
Scott, A. W., M.A. (Dub.), Professor of Physical Science, St. David's College, Lampeter, South Wales.
Stewart, John Huston, B.A., F.R.U.I., B.Sc. (London); Professor of Experimental Physics, University College, Dublin.

CHEMISTRY.

Adeney, Walter E., F.I.C., A.R.C.Sc.I.
Bell, Chichester, M.B. (Dub.), Sen. Mod., T.C.D.
Campbell, John, M.E. (Dub.), F.R.U.I., Professor, University Coll., Dub.
Davy, Edmund W., M.A., M.D. (Dub.)
Dixon, Augustus E., M.D., F.C.S., Prof. of Chemistry, Queen's Coll., Cork.
Falkiner, Niclan M., M.B., M.Ch. (Dub.), F.O.S.I.
Lappar, Edwin, L.K.Q.C.P.I., Lec. in Chem., Ledwich School of Medicine.
Leitz, Edmund A., Ph.D., F.C.S., Prof. of Chemistry, Queen's Coll., Belfast.
Macmillan, John, Laboratory, Royal College of Surgeons, Ireland.
M'Hugh, Michael, M.B. (Dub.), Senior Mod., T.C.D.
Moss, Richard J., F.C.S., F.I.C., Registrar and Chemical Analyst, Royal Dublin Society.
Pratt, J. Dallas, M.A., M.D.
Reynolds, James Emerson, M.D. (Dub.), F.R.S., Professor of Chemistry, University of Dublin.
Robertson, Mary W., M.A. (R.U.I.)
Werner, Emil A., F.C.S.

BOTANY.

Anderson, R. J., M.A., M.D. (R.U.I.), Prof. of Nat. Hist., Queen's Coll., Galway.
Boulger, G. S., F.L.S., F.G.S.
Dixon, Henry H., B.A., Sen. Mod., T.C.D.
Hartog, Marcus M., M.A., D.Sc., F.L.S., F.R.U.I., Prof. Nat. Hist., Queen's College, Cork.
Melville, Alex. G., M.D. (Edin.), M.R.C.S.E., Ex-Professor of Natural History, Queen's College, Galway.

Pim, Greenwood, M.A. (Dub.), Sen. Mod., T.C.D.
Sigerson, George, M.D., M.CH. (R.U.I.)
Wilson, Andrew, PH.D., F.R.S.E., F.L.S.
Wright, Ed. Perceval, M.D. (Dub.), Professor of Botany, University of
Dublin.

DRAWING

Atkinson, George M., Exam., Science and Art Dept., South Kensington.
Bowler, H. A., Inspector and Assist. Director, Art Division, Science and
Art Department, South Kensington.
Carroll, John, Art Master, Hammersmith Training Coll.
Conan, Florence.
Crainer, Walter, Head Master, Government School of Art, Stevenson
Memorial Hall, Chesterfield.
Crowther, W. E.
Harris, Robert, Art Master, St. Paul's School, London.
Jackson, Joshua, Art Master, Manchester Grammar School.
Keogh, Alice M.
Langman, A. W. F., Senior Drawing Inspector to the London School
Board.
Lindsay, Thomas M., Drawing Master, Rugby School.
O'Brien, Edward Stewart, B.A., B.E. (R.U.I.)
Prendergast, P. J., C.E.
Rawle, John S., F.S.A.
Scully, T., B.E. (R.U.I.)
Vinter, J. A., London.

THEORY OF MUSIC

Allison, H., MUS.D. (Dub.)
Elliott, Stanislaus.
Garrett, George, MUS.D., M.A. (Cantab.)
Gater, William H., B.A., MUS.D. (Dub.)
Gick, Thomas, MUS.D. (Dub.)
Goodwin, W. G.
Hanrahy, J. H.
Hoffmann, F.
Houghton, Edward.
Joab, T. R. G., MUS.D. (Dub.)
Karbusch, L., MUS.D. (Dub.)
Malone, Robert, MUS.D. (Dub.)
Marks, J. Chr., MUS.D. (Oxon.)
Marks, T. Osborne, MUS.D.
Muntz, Ellis.
Rogers, Brendan J.
Seymour, Joseph, MUS.B.
Smith, Joseph, MUS.D. (Dub.)
Taylor, Charlotte M., MUS.B. (R.U.I.)

DOMESTIC ECONOMY.

Barlow, Jane.
Barrington-Ward, M. J., M.A. (Oxon.), H. M. Inspector of Schools.
Gallaher, Fannie M.
Harrison, W. Jerome, Science Demonstrator, Birmingham School
Board, &c.
Moore, Louisa.
Todd, Mary B.

SHORTHAND.

Holt, Henry.
Hunt, Henry.
Ryan, Charles.

APPENDIX II.

LIST OF EXAMINERS

SELECTED, WITH THE APPROVAL OF THE LORD LIEUTENANT, TO CONDUCT THE EXAMINATIONS IN 1894.

GREEK AND LATIN.

Dougan, T. W., M.A., Ex-Fellow, St. John's College, Cambridge, Professor of Latin, Queen's College, Belfast.
Doyle, Charles F., M.A. (R.U.I.), B.A. (Dub.), Sen. Mod., T.C.D.
Kelly, Very Rev. J. J., Canon.
Kerin, R. G. R., B.A. (London).
Maguire, Rev. E., Professor of Classics, St. Patrick's College, Maynooth.
Molohan, John P., B.A. (Dub.), Sen. Mod., T.C.D.
Montgomery, Robert, M.A., University Student (R.U.I.), M.A., 1st Class Classical Tripos, Cantab.
Morgan, Rev. W. Moore, M.A., T.C.D.
Rine, Rev. James, B.D. (Dub.)
Wilkins, Rev. George, M.A. (Dub.), F.T.C.D.
Wilson, Herbert, B.A. (Dub.), 1st Sen. Mod., T.C.D.

ENGLISH.

Barry, Rev. Louis Aug., LL.D. (Dub.)
Clancy, Rev. John J., Professor of English Literature, St. Patrick's College, Maynooth.
Colclough, John D.
Croly, D., M.A. (R.U.I.), Professor of English Literature, Catholic Training College, Drumcondra.
Dixon, W. M., B.A., LL.B., 1st Sen. Mod., T.C.D.
Evans, Rev. Henry, D.D.
Henry, Rev. J. Edgar, M.A. (R.U.I.)
Joyce, P. W., LL.D., Ex-Professor, Board of National Education.
Macran, Henry S., M.A., F.T.C.D.
Maguennis, William, M.A., F.R.U.I.
Nicolls, Archibald J., LL.B. (Dub.)
Owens, Rev. S., St. Patrick's College, Maynooth.
Park, John, M.A. (R.U.I.), F.R.U.I., Professor of Logic and Metaphysics, Queen's College, Belfast.
Story, Mary, M.A., University Student, R.U.I.
Taylor, John F., B.A.

FRENCH.

Amours, F. J., B. ès L., French Master, Glasgow Academy.
Barbier, Georges E., Lecturer in French, The Athenæum, Glasgow.
Cogery, A., B.A., LL. (Paris), Examiner in French, Trinity College, London.
Hogan, Rev. J. F., St. Patrick's College, Maynooth.
Jansu, Elphege, Assistant Examiner in the University of London.
Oger, V., French Lecturer, Univ. Coll., Liverpool.
Spencer, Frederic, M.A., PH.D., Professor of Modern Languages, University College, Bangor.

GERMAN.

Steinberger, Valentine, M.A. (R.U.I.), Professor of Modern Languages, Queen's College, Galway.

SPANISH.

Steinberger, Valentine, M.A. (R.U.I.), Professor of Modern Languages, Queen's College, Galway.

ITALIAN.

Farinelli, A. Professor of Italian, University College, London.

CELTIC.

Murphy, Rev. James E. H., M.A., (Dublin), Ex-Sis., Bedell Sch., T.C.D.

MATHEMATICS.

Fry, M. W. Joseph, B.A. (Dub.), F.T.C.D.

Griffin, Gerald.

Inwood, Thomas W., B.A., Professor of Mathematics, St. Gregory's College, Downside, Bath.

Johnston, J. P., M.A. (Dub.), Sen. Mod., T.C.D.

Johnston, Swift P., M.A. (Dub.), 1st Sen. Mod., T.C.D., Univ. Student.

Joly, C. J., M.A., 1st Sen. Mod., University Student, T.C.D.

Kelly, Patrick.

Lennon, Rev. Francis, D.D., Professor of Mathematics and Natural Philosophy, St. Patrick's College, Maynooth.

M'Weeney, Henry C., M.A. (R.U.I.), Sen. Mod. (T.C.D.)

Orr, Wm. M'F., M.A. (R.U.I.), Sen. Wrangler, Fellow of St. John's College, Cambridge; Professor of Applied Mathematics and Mechanism, Royal College of Science, Ireland.

Power, Rev. Thos. R., Prof. of Mathematics, St. Patrick's Coll., Thurles.

Rea, James C., B.A. (R.U.I.), Professor in the Church of Ireland Training College, Kildare-place.

ARITHMETIC AND BOOK-KEEPING.

Dowd, Rev. James, B.A. (Dub.), Sen. Mod., T.C.D.

Dowling, P. A. E., B.A.

Keoghan, Rev. Patrick, B.A. (R.U.I.)

Whitten, Fredrick A., Accountant, Representative Church Body.

NATURAL PHILOSOPHY.

Coffey, George, B.E. (Dub.)

Joly, John, D.SC., F.R.S.

CHEMISTRY.

Letts, Edmund A., PH.D., F.C.S., Prof. of Chemistry, Queen's College, Belfast.

BOTANY.

Sigerson, George, M.D., M.CH. (R.U.I.)

DRAWING.

Carroll, John, Art Master, Hammersmith Training College.

Crowther, W. E.

Keogh, Alice M.

O'Brien, Edward Stewart, B.A., B.E. (R.U.I.)

THEORY OF MUSIC.

Gick, Thomas, MUS.D. (Dub.)

DOMESTIC ECONOMY.

Gallaher, Fannie M.

Todd, Mary B.

SHORTHAND.

Holt, Henry, B.L.

Ryan, Charles.

APPENDIX III.

EXTRACTS FROM THE REPORTS OF THE EXAMINERS, 1894.

GREEK.

SENIOR GRADE.—FIRST PAPER.—BOYS.

Report of J. P. MOLOHAN.

The result of the examination of the First Greek Paper of the Boys of the Senior Grade is highly satisfactory.

The questions in grammar—accidence, accentuation, and syntax—were answered creditably.

The composition, on the whole, was well done. The renderings of many of the candidates were admirable, both for grammatical accuracy and the employment of correct idioms. This showed that these candidates had studied the prescribed prose author—Demosthenes, Olynthiacs—with a view, not only to learning the translation, but to mastering the Greek phrases and expressions characteristic of Demosthenes. It would lighten the labours of the Examiners, if the student, when making several copies of the composition, would cross out all except the one by which he elects to be judged.

The passages from the Olynthiacs were translated into vigorous and idiomatic English. A large proportion of the candidates obtained nearly full marks for translation. The answers to No. 11—questions arising out of the subject-matter of the author—were not so satisfactory.

I have much pleasure in adding that most of the papers were neat, and the answers carefully arranged, showing, in this respect, a marked improvement over the Greek papers of the same grade that I examined last year.

SENIOR GRADE.—SECOND PAPER.—BOYS.

Report of T. W. DOUGAN.

The answering of the candidates on this paper is, on the whole, very satisfactory. Decidedly weak papers are few. As a rule, candidates have not neglected any part of the paper. There seemed to be a more intimate acquaintance with the text of the prescribed author than I have found on previous occasions.

The answers to part (b) of the question upon metre were the most disappointing portion of the work. It is very evident that few of the candidates know what a *caesura* is. The verse passage for unseen translation was, as usually happens, better done than the prose passage.

I should recommend candidates to read over, from time to time, a few pages of their prescribed prose subject which they have previously carefully prepared. They should read it at the same rate of speed as they would an English history or speech. This will imperceptibly cause the prose rhythm to steal into their minds, and greatly improve both their composition and their unseen translation.

MIDDLE GRADE.—FIRST PAPER.—BOYS.

Report of J. P. MOLOHAN.

The work sent up by the Boys of the Middle Grade in answer to the questions set on this paper was excellent alike in grammar, composition, translation, the subject matter of the author, and scansion. There were very few "blank" papers, and not many written in a careless manner.

The question in grammar which gave most trouble to the weaker candidates was No. 1, that on the declension of nouns.

When selecting the sentences for composition, the examiners, while avoiding a direct translation, adapted these sentences from the prose work set for this grade—Plato, The Apology of Socrates—and they did so, to see how far the students had devoted themselves to an intelligent study of their author. The result is one, on which both teachers and students deserve the warmest congratulation. The compositions showed not only a good knowledge of the laws of Greek construction and accentuation, but in many cases the phraseology was identical with that of Plato. Some candidates gave alternative renderings of the sentences. It would be better, in my opinion, to give only one.

The translation into English was capital, both as regards accuracy and style. A large number quoted quite correctly the lines asked in No. 9, while there were very few that did not make a fairly successful attempt at quoting them. The scansion question was also well answered, and the peculiarities noticed by most of the candidates.

MIDDLE GRADE.—SECOND PAPER.—BOYS.

Report of B. C. B. KEELY, B.A., and J. P. MOLOHAN, M.A.

We consider that the answering in this paper reflects great credit on the candidates and the schools that prepared them. The translation of the Plato was excellent. Many candidates, however, displayed ignorance of the Greek particles, translating them indiscriminately by "indeed," or "at least," without regard to the sense. Passage A was done exceedingly well by nearly everybody. Passage B proved a stumbling-block to several, who failed to grasp the force of ωσοτας, ελευτερο, ϕυαν, and ϕευ̉ειν with the future participle. The questions on the subject matter were admirably answered. Question 3, which dealt with the parsing of words occurring in the author, was not quite so satisfactory. The translation at sight was, on the whole, very good, and showed that the candidates had been well trained. The history was weak, generally speaking; in some cases the questions were not tried at all. There were, however, some excellent papers, in which the questions were answered in a clear and concise manner. Candidates, even when they are certain of its correctness, should guard against giving information which is not required by the examiner. For instance, some when asked to give the life of Alexander the Great from his accession to the invasion of Persia, gave either a full account of his father's career, or of the conquest of Persia.

We are glad to be able to add that the general neatness of the papers deserves special commendation.

JUNIOR GRADE.—FIRST PAPER.—BOYS AND GIRLS.

Report of Rev. GEORGE WILKINS, M.A.

(a) The answering in Greek of the Junior Grade candidates contrasted favourably with the answering in Latin of those Junior Grade candidates whom I examined. It was more intelligent in every way. But though the efforts made to master the grammar had been admirable, the learning of the irregular verbs had evidently proved too difficult a task for many of the boys, and therefore, of course, they were weak in composition. All, however, made some attempt to compose, and many succeeded brilliantly.

(b) It is absolutely necessary to continue the use of the "word for word" translation, as a touchstone of intelligent mastery of the prescribed author. Some candidates, beyond all doubt, learn "a translation" by heart, trusting to the chance of recognising some word which may serve as a cue to set them going. The best boys gave the ordo verborum and the translation in parallel columns; obviously, the most intelligent arrangement and the clearest to the sight.

JUNIOR GRADE.—SECOND PAPER.—BOYS.

Report of T. W. DOUGAN.

I have examined the work of the candidates in Greek of the Junior Grade.

The second piece of prepared translation was better done than the first, many candidates appearing not to collect their thoughts until they had been some time in the Examination room. It happened in rather many cases that candidates who did badly upon the prescribed author got high marks for unseen translation. On the other hand it was seldom found that those who did well upon the prescribed author broke down in unseen translation. This was due, I suspect, to the fact that candidates, being aware that translation at sight is marked very high, took special care to do their best upon it; their teachers, however, would do well to warn them that the marks allotted to prepared work are far too high to be thrown away.

There was a small percentage of candidates who did nothing whatever in the examination, being present, it would seem, in the examination room through no choice of their own. This number, however, was very much lower than when I examined eight or nine years ago.

There was a larger, though not an absolutely large, percentage of candidates whose teachers would evidently have done better to have prepared them for the Preparatory Grade. These candidates, in many

instances, displayed the spectacle of a boy struggling manfully with a
subject which was quite beyond his capacity. They very commonly
gave the impression that they were doing their very best, and yet they
produced very little result.

I think that teachers generally admit that it pays well to spend time
ungrudgingly in mastering the elementary work, and I am convinced
that when this is done the pupil who has any aptitude for the subject
will advance by leaps and bounds, and soon leave behind those who
have been hurried forward into higher classes before they had any
accurate knowledge of the lower work.

Preparatory Grade.—First Paper.—Boys and Girls.

Report of Rev. George Wilkins, M.A.

From the answering it appeared clear that a knowledge of the
whole Greek Grammar is too much to expect from the rank and file of
boys and girls in the Preparatory Grade. As soon as they reached the
questions on the verbs, many candidates who had shown thorough
mastery of the earlier portions of the grammar, were quite out of their
depth, and of course in the Composition were utterly at sea. From the
painstaking character of the answering of the rank and file, and the
really admirable answering of the others, it was plain that both students
and teachers had done their best, but owing to the intrinsic difficulties
of the great task set them, and perhaps to the number of rival subjects
studied concurrently, a large proportion were unable to conquer their
work completely. This indicates no falling off in the study of Greek;
the report of last year tallies with this year's tale, and seems to show
that the whole grammar (with Composition exemplifying its rules) is
a task too severe for any but exceptionally clever boys and girls of this
grade.

The girls showed such uncertainty with regard to the use of the
aspirate and the *iota subscriptum* that some defect in their teaching
may be presumed.

Preparatory Grade.—Second Paper.—Boys and Girls.

Report of Rev. E. Maguire, D.D.

The " word for word " translation was almost everything that could
be desired. Obviously, this element of the examination receives exceptional attention. Only one question, embracing two passages, and
carrying a pretty high maximum of marks, was proposed to be so
rendered ; and it is satisfactory to record that from 80 to 95 per cent.
was not an unusual award, while many scored full marks. Indeed, the
tendency on the part of the pupils this year, was to extend this form
of translating far beyond the prescribed limits, to the bewildering em-
barrassment of the examiner. Many answer books presented the
dismembered parts of a kind of mosaic-work, very difficult to put

together. The writers of such papers either carried in their minds throughout the idea impressed on them by constant practice, that they should give the Greek word first and its English equivalent immediately after; or, their primary aim was to make the most of the passage before them, and they studiously wrote down the Greek word, even where they knew it was not asked for, to show that they had a knowledge of the vocabulary, though they might have failed to master the full sense. Everybody knows the difficulty of making pupils under fourteen years comprehend, fully and precisely, the bearings of all the questions, however carefully they may be worded, on an examination paper, where they are crystallised in writing, and where repeated and cross examination is precluded by the very nature of the case. Unfortunately, or perhaps sometimes fortunately, for the candidates, the examiners cannot even take into consideration the impression made by the general tone of an answer-book. They must follow rightly the legal principle of attending only to the "*allegata et probata.*"

The following hint will appear rather hackneyed, but it is the very reverse of superfluous:—*Candidates ought to read over with keen attention the entire examination paper before they begin to write their answer to any question.* Time occupied in trying to understand in what mould precisely the answers are to be cast, is very far from being wasted. First thoughts, which do not commend themselves as entirely free from doubt, may be securely committed to the back of the page as "rough work," where they cannot in any way influence the examiner.

Two other features conspicuous in the Answer-books, viewed as a whole, deserve special comment. The "Translation at Sight" was marvellously well done by a comparatively large number of the candidates, while an exceptionally small percentage failed to attempt it, with a fair amount of success. This is a progressive stride, which my experience had not prepared me to expect. Again, the number of total failures threatens soon to reach zero. Evidently, neither teacher nor pupil regards the small "f" of the Pamphlet as possessing any attractive charm.

The answers in History and Geography were a vast improvement on those of last year.

SENIOR GRADE.—FIRST PAPER.—GIRLS.

Report of J. P. MOLOHAN.

The answering of the Girls on this paper does not call for any comment other than what I have made on the Boys. It is creditable that all the Girl candidates have passed.

SENIOR GRADE.—SECOND PAPER.—GIRLS.

Report of T. W. DOUGAN.

I have examined the work of six girls upon this paper. One of these candidates did really good work, the other five did very fairly. The remarks which I have made in detail about the answering of the boys on this paper apply also to the answering of the girls.

Many candidates have a tendency to write answers upon points to which the question does not refer (and girls seem more prone than boys to do this). For instance, several candidates, boys and girls, wrote at great length a description of the circumstances in which Demosthenes died—the *causes which led to* his death were asked for. Similarly the *constitutions* of the Achaean and Aetolian Leagues were to be described—a number of histories of these two leagues were given.

The examiner can scarcely give marks in such a case, while the candidate usually loses time and fails to complete the paper.

MIDDLE GRADE.—FIRST PAPER.—GIRLS.

Report of J. P. MOLOHAN.

The remarks which I have made on the Boys are equally applicable to the Girls. I wish, however, to notice that the answering of the candidates who has obtained highest marks amongst the Girls falls little short of that of the best of the Boys.

MIDDLE GRADE.—SECOND PAPER.—GIRLS.

Report of J. P. MOLOHAN.

The answering of the three Girls who presented themselves for examination in this paper was good, with the exception of the history. The translation of the Apology of Socrates and the grammar were fairly known, and the answers to the questions on the subject matter of the author were still better. I wish to draw particular attention to the excellence of the translation at sight, which shows that these students have acquired a sound knowledge of Greek. The history questions were scarcely attempted. This is to be regretted, as, with a little application to this branch of the programme, these candidates, who did so well in the rest of the work, were bound to score highly in the history also.

JUNIOR GRADE.—SECOND PAPER.—GIRLS.

Report of T. W. DOUGAN.

I have examined fifteen girls in this grade. Of these, one gained very high marks, four or five gained high marks, while five or six were marked very low.

The remarks which I have made about the answering of the boys of this grade apply also to the answering of the girls, and the following remarks apply to the work of the boys just as much as to that of the girls.

It appears to me to be at once one of the most important and one of the most irksome parts of the teacher's duty to insist on receiving from his pupil a translation which is good English and makes good sense,

The beginner scarcely realises that the passages he is translating have
a satisfactory meaning, while the teacher is often very well satisfied if
the pupil knows the meaning of the individual words, and does not
show himself very critical as to how these meanings are tacked together.
A slovenly habit is apt to be developed by the pupil in consequence,
and to stick to him throughout his course.

One of the many advantages to be looked for from a classical
education I take to be the improvement of the student's command of the
English language. This advantage will certainly be missed if the pupil
is allowed to translate into a jargon which is not English, although it
may sound familiar to his wearied and bilingual instructor. An
examiner in Greek will scarcely criticise the English set before him as
severely as he would if he were an examiner in English. But still,
when he calls for " Translation into English " he has a right to insist on
having the simple rules of English syntax observed, a clear sense
conveyed by each sentence, and the sentences within each period connected with one another by suitable connecting particles. A certain
number of candidates, many of them evidently possessing considerable
knowledge of Greek, work on a totally different principle, appearing to
think that a rough indication of the line of thought by means of
jerky and unconnected clauses suffices.

The task of reproducing the exact effect of a paragraph written in
an ancient inflected language, by means of a paragraph in a modern un-
inflected language, involving, as it often does, a rearrangement of
several of the clauses to be translated, necessarily exercises and develops
the student's powers of expression. The pupil who has been allowed to
work on the principle indicated above misses all this advantage. His
classical education has in fact been neglected. But to outsiders who
are unaware of the circumstances, his defects will probably serve as
arguments against the study of classics.

LATIN.

SENIOR GRADE.—FIRST PAPER.—BOYS.

Report of CHARLES F. DOYLE, M.A.

This paper comprised questions in Grammar, passages for Prose and
Verse Composition and an examination in Livy, Book V.

The answering on the Grammar portion of the paper was on the whole
good, and in many cases very good, but a large number of the candidates
seemed wholly unable to utilise their knowledge of Grammar in the
translation from English into Latin Prose. This would seem to point
to a want of practice in Latin Composition and an insufficient appre-
ciation by students of the object of learning Grammar. I had occasion
to make somewhat similar remarks about the answering in the Junior
Grade last year. Of course these observations must not be taken to be
of anything approaching to universal application as there were among
the answers many instances of really good compositions, and many
others of what would have been really good compositions but for the
occurrence of two or three stupid errors.

Hardly any candidate attempted the Verse Composition, and no
candidate obtained more than 20 marks in it (out of a total of 75).

The Livy was well known and had evidently been carefully prepared.

Several of the candidates, and some of them among the best, adopted the highly inconvenient practice of writing two copies of the Composition and leaving both open to examination. This may have arisen from mere forgetfulness to cancel the first, though in one or two cases the first was slightly the better of the two.

Senior Grade.—Second Paper.—Boys.

Report of Rev. E. Maguire, D.D.

The idea uppermost in my mind, on sitting down to report on the answer-books in this department, is that in the case of the vast majority of average boys, entirely too much attention has been given to mere verbal translation. This, no doubt, indicates the expenditure of a great deal of time and mental energy, and claims a commensurate acknow-ledgment in the form of marks; nor can such a mode of preparation be condemned on the ground that it is impolitic for present purposes on the part of pupil or school. Moreover, it is the highest level of develop-ment that 30 per cent. of the candidates could reasonably aspire to. But I think I am justified in suggesting that in the Senior Grade the sense, over and beyond the mere words, should command closer inspec-tion. The notable fact that the really brilliant students have abandoned all stereotyped forms of translation, and have proved their intimate acquaintance with the language by rendering the passages from unprescribed authors or works, almost as accurately as those called from the books set forth in the programme, encourages me to express a view that many esteemed teachers and examiners may dissent from. Indeed, I should be sorry that my suggestion would be acted on beyond reasonable limits. Where a candidate writes down the correct translation, the examiner must give full marks.

Pupils ought to be taught to cultivate precision in their answers. The system of periodic examinations, on the lines of the June Inter-mediate papers, is highly commendable. Quite a number of students, whose answering is admirable in parts, and who never come within view of the nadir of ignorance by any possibility, express themselves in an unconsidered and slovenly fashion. For instance; the following is a casual illustration of what I wish to convey, not specially selected, and the work of a student who scores pretty high marks:—" The Pantheon was a temple where all the gods were kept." The reader would imagine it was a kind of menagerie.

Another point I wish to call attention to, is the Prosody. It is not an uncommon thing to encounter an answer-book giving merely the quantities of all the syllables in the defined stanza. How could any marks be assigned in such cases? What is asked for is the *scansion*, and unless that is given, no credit can be awarded. Many add that the metre is Alcaic. Quite right! But where is the *scansion*? Above all the metres Horace employs, the Alcaic predominates, and there is no excuse for failing to give a good account of it.

MIDDLE GRADE.—FIRST PAPER.—BOYS.

Report of ROBERT MONTGOMERY, M.A.

Although very few of the candidates in this grade failed **utterly, yet** the answering cannot be regarded as entirely satisfactory.

While many of the students scored very high marks in grammar, a goodly number exhibited lamentable weakness in this part of the subject. The accidence was, on the whole, fair; but the syntax left much to be desired. In turning the passage from Cicero into *Oratio Obliqua*, only a small proportion of students seemed to understand clearly what they were doing, the majority seeming to consider it quite sufficient to scatter subjunctives about freely.

One part of the paper which was very unsatisfactory was the answering of the prosody questions, most of the candidates it is true succeeded in scanning the lines, or at least part of them; but this was obviously done in a haphazard kind of manner, as was shown when the writer attempted to explain the line by notes. In the first part of the question, where candidates were asked to distinguish the meanings of a few simple words according to the quantity of the important vowels, a painful want of knowledge was exhibited, and one could not help feeling that there were but few boys in this grade who could read a short piece of Latin text without hurting the feelings of a person sensitive about false quantities. This is a point which shows scholarship, or the lack of it, but in a written examination it is not very paying, and therefore seems to be wholly neglected in most of our schools.

It is impossible to praise the composition. About ten per cent. of the candidates did the short sentences excellently, and wrote very creditable continuous prose, but in most cases the Latin was simply a succession of painful blunders, showing an utter disregard of concord, sequence of tenses, or any of the ordinary grammatical rules.

The verse composition was conspicuous by its absence; only about half a dozen boys took any notice of it at all, and of these two or three were fairly successful. The piece selected was so easy, and the paraphrase so full, that any boy who had the faintest knowledge of prosody ought to have been able to make something out of it.

The most satisfactory part of the paper was the Cicero: for this I have nothing but praise; not only were the extracts well translated, but the questions on the subject matter, and on the various phrases requiring explanation, were answered in such a manner as to show clearly that this part of the subject had been carefully and intelligently studied.

It is quite evident that the greatest amount of attention is bestowed on the translation. This is, of course, as it should be, but still, if boys are to make any pretensions to Latin scholarship, other subjects ought not to be entirely neglected.

It is too common in Irish schools to find that the teaching of Latin composition consists in running rapidly over a few sentences at the beginning of the period devoted to Latin, the boys moving out what is wrong without knowing clearly why it is wrong, while all parties are hurrying on to the translation, as the real work of the hour. Teachers should be recommended to devote more time and care to the teaching of syntax combined with composition; this ought to be done by oral as well as written examination, accompanied by lucid demonstrations of the constructions on the black board. The result of the present system is, that boys have a hazy idea that a phrase like ' there is no doubt that ' ought to have some word beginning with ' *dum* ' followed by the word ' *quia*,' but are quite unable to carry the construction any further ; while in the case of the ' ablative absolute ' most boys seem to imagine that this much abused idiom ought to be dragged in every time they come across the word ' *having*.'

MIDDLE GRADE.—SECOND PAPER.—BOYS.

Report of HERBERT WILSON, B.A.

The answering on the whole was very good, with the qualification that there were evident signs of a very large percentage of the candidates having learnt by heart the translation of the prescribed book.

Some of the candidates translated the passage for translation at sight remarkably well ; the verse passage, however, appears to have been found somewhat difficult by the majority of the candidates.

JUNIOR GRADE.—FIRST PAPER.—BOYS.

Report of ROBERT MONTGOMERY, M.A.; REV. W. MOORE MORGAN, LL.D.; REV. JAMES RICE, B.D.; REV. GEORGE WILKINS, B.D.

In Accidence the results are disappointing—less satisfactory than in 1893. Surprisingly few boys could give the gen. sing. of *pater* or the perf. subj. of *cedo*. The knowledge of the numerals was very limited, and in many of the answers to question 2 there was a lamentable disregard of the second concord.

In Syntax many answered fairly, the difficulties in question 3 (equivalents for English prepositions) being very creditably dealt with by a large number.

The Compositions were somewhat better than those of the Junior Grade last year. About one-fifth of this year's candidates have scored over 65 per cent., while nearly the same number have failed altogether. In many cases knowledge of constructions has been neutralised by gross violations of the simplest concords. On the other hand, boys who showed no idea of the government of sentences had got hold of stock phrases like "*certior fieri*" and "*non dubium est quin*," while unable to produce better Latin than "*ducem certior facti sunt*," "*juvenes me scripsit multas epistolas*." We would strongly urge teachers to insist on much closer attention to the *simplest* rules of Syntax.

The translations were, on the whole, very fairly done. There is the usual evidence of slovenly and inaccurate work, especially in the rendering of the long sentence in passage C. What has been said about the "word for word" translation of Greek holds good of Latin also : *supra* p. 9 (5). Many boys went absurdly astray in the "word for word" translation who gave the English of the rest of passage A correctly. Still, on the whole, the translations from Cæsar were more satisfactory than those from Cornelius Nepos in 1893.

JUNIOR GRADE.—SECOND PAPER.—BOYS.

Report of R. C. B. KERIN, B.A.; Rev. E. MAGUIRE, D.D.; HERBERT WILSON, M.A.

We have much pleasure in stating that the papers, on the whole, were very creditably answered, and that a large number of answer-books showed marked excellence. The translation from Virgil was exceedingly accurate; but, as almost invariably happens, many candidates, by reproducing in the exact words, easily recognisable forms from English notes and translation books, proved that their work was more or less mechanical.

This habit of inserting explanations of obscure words or phrases, in the middle of the English rendering, must disturb the continuity to some extent; it is much more satisfactory to reserve such remarks for the end of the passage in question.

With these trivial limitations, we are glad to report that the work of translating showed abundant evidence of industry and intelligence.

The answers to the Grammar questions from the author were excellent in very many cases; some candidates left nothing to be desired in the way in which they discussed the syntactical difficulties they had to deal with.

An unusually large percentage of the answer books showed great success in the rendering of the first passage for translation at sight; the second passage presented greater difficulty.

The results in the History examination are very gratifying; but, unimportant facts are frequently dwelt on at an unnecessary length. This was specially evident in the case of the last question. ("State briefly what you know concerning Fabius Cunctator and Cato.")

PREPARATORY GRADE (BOYS).—FIRST PAPER.

Report of CHARLES F. DOYLE, M.A., and Rev. W. MOORE MORGAN, LL.D.

A large number of the candidates answered the Accidence questions (1, 2, 3,) very fully and accurately. This applies especially to the conjugation of the verbs in question 3, which were rather out of the beaten track.

The same cannot be said of the answers to the questions on Syntax. Very few attempted question 6, and clear answers to question 5, (a) and (b), were rare.

More pains seem to have been taken with the Composition. In some cases the exercises were very well done, and few left them altogether untried.

The translations from Cæsar were in several cases extremely good, and showed careful and intelligent preparation; there were very few traces of the committal to memory of the English version so often noticed when prescribed portions are short. This would seem to indicate the advantage of "selections" over continuous portions of authors for junior students, as rendering the use of translations (so fatal to all beginners) much less likely. More intelligence was shown in the "word for word" translation (8, a) than in the corresponding work of the Junior Grade Boys.

In most cases the papers were neatly written, and the spelling was good.

E

PREPARATORY GRADE.—SECOND PAPER.—BOYS.

Report of Very Rev. J. J. KELLY and JOHN P. MOLOHAN.

The passages from Ovid were, on the whole, well translated, but when we found the inability to conjugate the verbs and decline the nouns occurring in these passages, and the ignorance of elementary syntax shown in answering question 2, by several candidates who translated fairly well, we were forced to conclude that, in these cases, the translation had been got up from printed English versions, and afforded no proof of any sound knowledge of the rudiments of the language. We think it would be well regularly to require the pupils to parse every word in a passage fully and accurately, and not merely those words which present some special difficulty. A considerable number seemed not to have prepared the selections from Ovid at all, and confined their study to Roman History, trusting to their general knowledge to answer questions in Syntax and translate at sight. We could not otherwise account for their poor attempts at translating the passages set, where the quantity to be prepared was so small. Yet we consider it showed a creditable knowledge of Latin that some of those who evidently had not prepared the Ovid at all, passed on the translation at sight, Syntax, and History Questions. Some seemed passed by answering in the prescribed book and the passage for translation at sight, while they seemed to have entirely neglected the Roman History, by some attention to which they could have passed with honours. Such answers as "Numa Pompilius built churches and monasteries", and "The Comitia Tributa was the first Plebeian Consul", are not satisfactory as the result of a year's study of the Outlines of Roman History. There were, however, some very good History papers, and the History, on the whole, was fairly known.

The attempts at the translation of the unprepared passage were generally weak, showing in many cases ignorance of the common concords, and the rudiments of Latin construction. Passages cannot be translated at sight without much labour and practice on the part of pupils, and continual instruction and correction on the part of teachers. There was a considerable number of "blanks."

We have pleasure in adding that a large proportion of the papers were neat and legible, and had the answers carefully arranged.

SENIOR GRADE.—FIRST PAPER.—GIRLS.

Report of CHARLES F. DOYLE.

The girls' compositions, though satisfactory, were (with one or two notable exceptions) not so good as the average of the boys', while their knowledge of the prescribed Book of Livy seemed more accurate and intelligent.

The observations made on the whole examination in my report on the boys' answering apply also to the answering of the girls.

SENIOR GRADE.—SECOND PAPER.—GIRLS.

Report of Rev. E. Maguire, D.D.

Forty-three girls presented themselves in this paper, and it is gratifying to be in a position to report that not even one out of the forty-three failed to secure the percentage of marks required for a pass in the subjects of the paper. Indeed, I find that the number who have not reached 50 per cent. is under five. Another striking fact is, that the girl who has got the highest award, scores precisely the same number of marks as the boy receiving highest marks from me—that is, 510 out of a maximum total of 570. As a rule, the " translation at sight " was not their strong point, but in the case of text-books, history, &c., they have shown that they possess much more retentive memories than the boys. The answering all round in this paper is decidedly the best I have ever encountered in any grade.

MIDDLE GRADE.—FIRST PAPER.—GIRLS.

Report of R. Montgomery, M.A.

The answering on this paper was fair, but the number of really good papers was comparatively small. As with the boys, the translation was the most satisfactory part of the work; with a few exceptions the syntax and the composition were very weak indeed. A large proportion of the candidates did not attempt the continuous prose at all, and only a very few were at all successful in their treatment of it. It is a pity that with girls so little attention is given to syntax and composition, which afford such an excellent training for the mind when properly studied; but it seems to be the case that most attention is devoted to a smattering of accidence, and the knowledge of an author which can be gained from a translation.

MIDDLE GRADE.—SECOND PAPER.—GIRLS.

Report of Herbert Wilson, B.A.

I examined seventy-seven of these papers, and found the answering on the whole excellent. The translation passages from the prescribed work were very well done by almost all the candidates. The parsing was rather weak.

My remarks on the same paper (for boys) as to the passages for translation at sight apply equally to the girls.

JUNIOR GRADE.—FIRST PAPER.—GIRLS.

Report of Rev. James Rice.

The general answering in Grammar and Composition was far from satisfactory. There was, however, a fair proportion of good papers, and some I would say were very good. The total disregard of the simplest rules of Syntax by the great majority of those examined was very observable, and the word for word translation was, in most cases, very poor. In fact, no attempt was made in these papers to make any kind of connected sense of the passage. The general translation of the passages selected was fairly well done on the whole.

I would strongly recommend that both teachers and pupils should be advised to devote more attention to the ordinary declensions of nouns and adjectives, the conjugations of the regular verbs, and the prepositions, with the cases they govern, before entering on the more difficult parts of Grammar. I think it is most desirable to secure, if possible, a sound fundamental knowledge of Grammar, and this, I believe, would be best done by encouraging pupils to pay more attention to the elementary parts of it.

JUNIOR GRADE.—SECOND PAPER.—GIRLS.

Report of THOMAS W. DOUGAN, M.A.

The general impression derived from reading the 245 sets of answers sent in by the girls of the Junior Grade was very favourable. Scarcely any blank or very weak papers were sent in, while some of the work was of a very high order.

I should however pronounce the average performance to have been respectably mediocre rather than brilliant.

The translation from the prescribed book of Virgil was well done. Careful preparation and honest work were abundantly indicated. If more candidates had possessed and used handy classical Atlases of their own there would have been more precision in the answering upon points of Geography.

The weakest work was shown in dealing with the question upon metre. Comparatively few were able to mark the scansion of an ordinary hexameter line free from metrical peculiarities, and yet (one of the few indications of cramming which I observed) a number who failed in this were prepared for the peculiarity of a line of *exceptional build*.

In Unseen Translation too many candidates proved wholly unable to deal with the construction of an ordinary sentence from Cæsar. It appears to me that teachers require in the first place to inform the average pupil that a translation from a Latin author, if correct, will make lucid sense, and in the second place, to prepare him or her for producing such translations by seeing that he or she clearly understands the *little words* of the sentence, especially the *connecting words*—conjunctions, pronouns, &c.

More candidates were successful with the unseen Verse extract (from Virgil), yet here the majority paid far too little regard to the ample information afforded to them by genders, numbers, and cases. Most of these ladies, for instance, transformed Iris into a young man, under the name of Irus, though the text eloquently opposed their proceedings.

These candidates did not neglect History. The average mark here was high. A minority of candidates furnished dates for nearly every event, and yet failed to give any further information. Knowledge so limited can scarcely improve the mind any more than it can satisfy the examiner.

PREPARATORY GRADE.—FIRST PAPER.—GIRLS.

Report of Rev. W. MOORE MORGAN, LL.D.

The answering in Accidence was satisfactory, quite as good as that of the boys in the same grade, but, as with the latter, Syntax was the weak point, and few did well in it.

The Composition results were indifferent; very few showed a clear idea of construction. Of the 175 girls examined, nearly one-fourth failed altogether in Composition, and only 11 scored more than 65 per cent. The translations from Cæsar were well done by a few, though strangely enough, some of the best overlooked the requirements of " word for word " translation altogether. There was evidence, in these cases, of a painstaking study of the prescribed selections. The majority, however, showed great neglect of the translation work. Very many failed altogether in the two longer passages; the wildest shots were often made, the English given having no apparent connexion with the original.

The questions on the author were, on the whole, well answered; in fact, several showed knowledge of these questions who failed entirely in translation.

PREPARATORY GRADE.—SECOND PAPER.—GIRLS.

Report of Very Rev. J. J. KELLY.

The answering of the girls was, on the whole, somewhat better than that of the boys. A somewhat larger percentage got pass marks on this paper. But that was to be expected, considering the difference in numbers. A great ignorance of parsing was shown by a large majority. The attempts at translating the unseen passage were, as a rule, wretched. No knowledge was shown of the agreement, dependence, or government of words, or the construction of sentences.

I would make here to teachers and pupils, the same suggestions as in the case of the boys, with regard to constant teaching, practice, and correction in parsing, and translating unseen passages.

ENGLISH

SENIOR GRADE.—FIRST PAPER.—BOYS.

Report of WILLIAM MAGENNIS, M.A.

With a few brilliant exceptions the Senior Grade compositions were disappointing. Many candidates elected to write on " Common Sense," and displayed a lamentable ignorance of what this term denotes. Commonplaces concerning success in life, anecdotes showing the stupidity of certain persons, and tame moralizings on life in general were the main constituents of these essays, and poverty of vocabulary their common characteristic. Those who selected the text from Bacon—" A Crowd is not Company "—were more successful; and it may fairly be said of some of them that they produced papers not unworthy of the lesser eighteenth century essayists. Equally high praise is due to a small number who discussed Goldsmith's estimate of Burke ; and the praise is due alike for form and for matter, both of which were admirable, not to say marvellous, considering the unfavourable conditions under which the compositions were written. Though the general level of excellence was not very high, it is satisfactory to note that in point of spelling and punctuation there is little or no room for dispraise.

The knowledge of grammar exhibited by the papers was fairly good. The question concerning the grammatical use or function of words in three passages from "Coriolanus" was somewhat insufficiently dealt with, and the same remark applies to those on elementary philology. Analysis seems a favourite study to judge from the remarkable ability with which nearly every candidate treated the question upon it ; and I may add that considerable neatness and skill were shown in the mode of tabulating adopted for the analysis.

Contrary to my expectation, the text and annotation of "Coriolanus" were not preferred to the æsthetic study of the drama ; indeed, as a rule, dramatic criticism was better attempted than the paraphrase or repetition of speeches. Memorising in this case was notably discarded in favour of original work, and the original work in not a few instances was of the highest merit. This is a circumstance that indicates the value and the character of the instruction in English Literature given in our Intermediate Schools, and reflects the utmost credit on the teachers.

SENIOR GRADE.—SECOND PAPER.—BOYS.

Report of JOHN F. TAYLOR, B.A.

The remarkable thing in the papers of the Senior Grade this year appears to me to be the level standard of accuracy in the answering, so that differences and inequalities arise more from the quantity of the work done than from difference in the value of the separate answers or fractional parts of answers. There are very few cases indeed, of wild guessing, and none at all of the pretended misunderstanding of questions, or of gratuitous answering of what is not asked. This seems to me a very good sign, as it shows that an intellectual conscience has been formed, and that false shows of answering have been found by experience to be of no avail. Method and care are shown in nearly all the answers, and the attention to mechanical details is very creditable and praiseworthy. When questions call for something more than accurate memory, the results are not very satisfactory, but taking the answering as a whole, I think the boys have worked honestly at the several subjects, trusting, no doubt, too much to mere verbal knowledge, but at the same time setting out that knowledge with clearness, directness, and accuracy.

MIDDLE GRADE.—FIRST PAPER.—BOYS.

Report of Rev. HENRY EVANS, D.D.

Beginning with composition, twenty-seven per cent. of the candidates wrote on "Life at the Equator," twenty-six per cent. on "The Influence of Literature on Social Life," and forty-seven per cent. on—

"Absence of occupation is not rest,
A mind quite vacant is a mind distrest,"

Few of the essays were brilliant; scarcely any were stupid. Generally speaking, the language was appropriate, the grammar correct, and the execution of the work neatly done. The chief faults of the compositions were want of originality, exaggerated assertion, excessive rehearsal of common episodes; and in the case of those who wrote on the second theme, an undue measure of quotation from the school manuals on literature.

The answering in *grammar* (with the exceptions mentioned hereafter), was not satisfactory. Many candidates seem not to have an idea of what is meant by "factitive object," or "retained object." The difference between the verbs *rise* and *raise*, *fall* and *fell*, was frequently not understood; on the other hand, it is right to say, that the distinction was excellently set forth by a considerable number.

The question, "what is a preposition, and what are the proper prepositions in use after certain given words?" although set for the first time this year, was one of the best answered on the Paper. The excellence of the answering, however, appears most in dealing with the second part of the question. The definitions given in reply to the first part reflect the confusing influence of the various manuals of English grammar used in the schools. Some of the candidates say "A preposition is a word which shows the relation of one *word* to another" (Smith and Hall), others say; "A preposition is a word which when placed before a noun or pronoun denotes some relation between the *things for which the words stand*" (Mason); some define a preposition as "a word prefixed to a *noun* or its equivalent to make up a qualifying or adverbial phrase" (Bain); others again say, "Prepositions are so named because they were formerly prefixed to the verb to modify its meaning" (Morris). These types of definition are here presented that teachers may see the necessity of preparing definitions for their own use, and configuring them to the function which words fulfil rather than deducing the function from the definition.

The parsing prescribed in question five was seldom well done. Few recognised *sweet* as an adjective in "the rose smells *sweet*," or apprehended the adverbial office of *fully* in "he is *fully* master of the subject." In "the rest were long to *tell*," the words in italics were mostly described as "a classical construction," and this was supposed to sufficiently illuminate the locution. I would fain point out the danger of using such language either in oral teaching or in annotating texts. To those who are learning English only, it can be no aid to say of a certain combination of words, that it is a "Latinism" or "a classical construction"; on the contrary, it is calculated to give a false sense of satisfaction, the pupil only too willingly acquiescing in what sounds to him as a learned explanation with which he ought to be content.

No part of the grammar section was so satisfactory as *analysis*. The alternative sentences were about equally chosen, and the work of analysing was generally done with marked intelligence. Of course there were failures, but even in these there was evidence of sound teaching. No matter what form was adopted, the analysis, as a rule, was made on right principles, and often with commendable thoroughness. Marked progress has undoubtedly been made in this department since I last examined.

Almost all the candidates show extensive acquaintance with *Paradise Lost*, Book I., and *Lycidas*. This year, as in former years, the questions which could be answered from mere memory of the text were usually well done; next to these, the candidates succeed best with such questions as may be answered from the notes to the school editions of Milton. I am happy, however, to report that the poems themselves, as classic specimens of English Literature, are better appreciated, their metrical structure better understood, and their literary charm more sensitively felt, than when I last examined in Milton. The question in metre and gnarios then set was not generally answered; this year it has been answered creditably by at least two-thirds of the candidates, and excellently by very many.

MIDDLE GRADE.—SECOND PAPER.—BOYS.

Report of HENRY S. MACRAE, M.A.

The answering in History and Geography Proper was on the whole satisfactory, and in many cases excellent. Macaulay's biographies, too, seemed to have been well prepared. But the answering in Physical Geography and English Literature was only poor. One might also mention that the ignorance of spelling and grammar displayed by some of the candidates was shocking.

With regard to Physical Geography, most of the candidates exhibited a complete lack of accurate terminology, which rendered the language of their answers so vague and general as to be well nigh unintelligible.

While it would be most undesirable to hamper candidates with regard to the order in which they answer the questions, one might suggest that they should be obliged to give the whole of their answer to any one question together, and not in different scraps in different **parts** of the answer-book.

JUNIOR GRADE.—FIRST PAPER.—BOYS.

Report of Rev. L. A. BARRY, LL.D.; W. MAGENNIS, M.A.; and MARK STONE, M.A.

The compositions, with some exceptions, lacked arrangement and a continuity of thought. Those on "Ulysses," for the most part consisted of extracts from Lamb, more or less accurately reproduced, but badly connected: the writers too frequently restricted themselves to a narrative of the hero's wanderings after the capture of Troy, and gave undue prominence to the incident in the cave of Polyphemus; indeed, not a few devoted as many as five pages to this alone. Many excellent essays were written on the subject of "Animal Pets," but the majority of the writers might have done better had they relied more on their own observation and experience. Some students who selected "Necessity is the Mother of Invention" as their theme, failed to grasp the real import of the sentence, and, identifying "necessity" with "poverty," laboured to prove that only the destitute can have any capacity for invention. As a rule, the compositions betrayed a want of training, and this not merely as regards the plan and structure, but even in respect of spelling and punctuation. A few displayed an entire ignorance of punctuation. Improper division into paragraphs, and eccentric punctuation and spelling, in many instances, detracted from otherwise good work. The confusion of "the" and "they," of "quiet" and "quite," the omission of verbs, the introduction of a second nominative where a dependent sentence intervenes between the first nominative and the predicate, the use of provincialisms such as "we do be," "I am just after," "for to," and the like: these are the commonest faults.

The answering in grammar was fairly good. Analysis, however, was not at all so well done as parsing, which in not a few cases was excellent.

The answers dealing with "The Lay of the Last Minstrel" showed intelligent study and thorough preparation; though it must be said that many candidates when asked to give the sense of certain passages in their own words neglected the meaning in favour of copious annotation and extraneous matter.

JUNIOR GRADE.—SECOND PAPER.—BOYS.

Report of Prof. J. EDGAR HENRY, M.A., JOHN F. TAYLOR, B.A.; and W. M. DIXON, M.A.

The papers show very much the same proportion of good answering, marked by the same excellence in memory and the same weakness in more general grasp of the subjects, which were noticed in the Report of last year. The want of method and care is as conspicuous as ever. The answers are jumbled and thrown out in the most irritating disorder. In many instances the answers are left unnumbered, and papers, other than those of the really good candidates, rarely show sufficient attention to detail. The feeblest pupil may be taught the principles of clearness and accuracy, which count for so much in after life. We are anxious to call attention once more to the illiteracy of many candidates who score high marks. We would suggest that specific provision should be made to enable an examiner to refuse full marks to a candidate who gives the information required by any question, but betrays an ignorance of the simplest principles of composition. We would also suggest that attention should be called on the answer books to the importance of assigning the correct numbers to all the answers together with their subdivisions, e.g. "Be careful to number each question and sub-division of questions you attempt. As far as possible give the full answer in one place."

The Geography of Ireland was well known, but **physical geography** seems to have been almost wholly neglected.

On the whole there is nothing to show improvement in dealing with matters involving a little reflection and judgment. The few questions which at all tested these qualities were as a rule but feebly attempted.

PREPARATORY GRADE.—FIRST PAPER.—BOYS.

Report of the Rev. J. J. CLANCY and P. W. JOYCE, LL.D.

We examined the boys of the Preparatory Grade, English, in Composition, Grammar, and Select Poetry.

(a) The Select Poetry was generally prepared with care. The candidates showed themselves well acquainted with the facts, and in this respect the answering was, on the whole, good. But much of this was mere mechanical memory-work; and when we came to test how far the candidates understood the context, the results were not quite so satisfactory. The last question in our paper asked for an explanation of four simple passages from the prescribed texts, and in this question there were more failures than in any other. It appears clear that explanation of context is, in some schools, very much neglected, and that the young students are not sufficiently exercised in thinking about the passages they read and get off by heart, and in giving their ideas in their own words as to meaning.

In regard to Composition, the candidates generally exhibited sufficient knowledge and imagination. The "Imaginary Balloon Voyage" afforded ample scope to those who had some knowledge of Geography and Natural History, and many of them availed themselves of the voyage with good results. A few had read Jules Verne and drew largely from him.

We feel bound to notice one commendable feature in the essays. The language used was generally simple and direct, as it ought to be, without any attempt at what is called fine writing. Some indeed were written in high-flown, grandiloquent language, but they were very few. A still smaller number bordered on flippancy or coarseness, both in ideas and words.

But the essays, while fully deserving these commendations, were very faulty in other important respects. They generally showed a lamentable absence of systematic training in what might be called the mechanical requisites of Composition. Punctuation commonly was very bad. Many wrote their essays with a succession of commas—a comma for everything—no other stop. Some used no stop of any kind, from beginning to end. Others, having some dim idea that they ought to punctuate in some way, threw in stops at random, without any discrimination—commas for periods, periods for commas and semicolons, &c. Not a few wrote out their memory-poetry without a stop of any kind, though expressly warned at head of question to pay particular attention to punctuation. Capital letters were managed as badly as punctuation; and many candidates had no idea of how to divide their discourse into sentences and paragraphs. In the simplest particulars many exhibited a want of training; particulars, simple indeed, but necessary to be attended to by all wishing to escape the charge of illiteracy. Some did not know how to strike out or insert words. Instead of running a line right through the rejected word, they enclosed it in a parenthesis, or underlined it, or overlined it. Others did not know the caret mark, or made it wrong, or turned it upside down, or on its side. Some were not taught to transcribe poetry, writing their poetical passages continuously, without any distinction of lines, prose fashion. The handwriting was generally plain and legible. Many, however, wrote a very bad unformed hand, difficult to make out—mere helpless scrawling. These children have tried to learn to write, but have not been taught.

To be able to write out a plain statement neatly and with moderate correctness, and to be able to understand and explain ordinary literary English—these two, so far as the written language is concerned, are what chiefly distinguish an educated from an illiterate person; yet these are the very parts of the course that seem to be most neglected.

A decided improvement in Grammar is needed. We found much inaccuracy in minute details, such as the position of the apostrophe in the possessive case. A great many failed to decline the words "ox," "goose," and "fly"; and some declined with six cases, after the Latin model, as if English had no grammar of its own. As regards parsing, many displayed a very lamentable want of knowledge, while some confounded the plainest parts of speech :—"'Toll for the brave': *Toll* a common noun, nominative case to the verb *brave.*"

The great majority of the candidates showed in their papers evident signs of training and preparation on the part of the teachers; these came from the good schools. But it is obvious that large numbers have been left very much to their own resources to prepare themselves for the examination as best they could, with little or no guidance from teachers. Hence, many wrote away at random, paying no attention to the directions on the question papers, and committing all sorts of blunders. Some, instead of parsing *ten* words, as they were asked to do, parsed *sixty*: some, instead of writing *one* of three pretty long passages, as directed, wrote out the whole three; and so forth. Many omitted even the numbers of the questions, and mixed up and scribbled their answers confusedly, in a manner quite unpresentable as a piece of English—a performance that a plain business man would laugh at; and it may be added, very perplexing and irritating to an Examiner. All this might be avoided by a little training on the part of the teachers; but probably some candidates presented themselves without the sanction of any teacher. To teach children to answer in writing, in proper form, a series of questions, is a valuable educational training; and—what indeed is of less consequence though not to be despised—is sure to add to the marks.

(*b.*) Our suggestions to teachers are obvious from the preceding.

(*c.*) It would be well, we think, if some plan were devised to encourage plain, open, legible handwriting, and to put down mere scribbling.

PREPARATORY GRADE.—SECOND PAPER.—BOYS.

Report of Rev. B. OWENS, and A. J. NICOLLS.

Speaking generally, the answering of the pupils whose papers were read by us was very satisfactory. A large majority of these boys showed a considerable amount of intelligence, and their careful training was manifested by the way in which they grasped the meaning of the questions. There was one strange exception; for a large proportion of the boys were unable to explain the simple terms "Latitude" and "Longitude." Apart from this, we found but few nonsensical answers; and a satisfactory number of the pupils who gained pass marks also reached the standard for honours on this paper.

We found a serious amount of wrong spelling, even in the papers of boys who were well prepared, in other respects, for the examination. Proper names were fearfully mutilated, and many words in frequent use were spelled as if the phonetic system had been adopted. The special preparation of talented pupils should not divert a teacher from insisting upon correct spelling as one of the essentials of sound education. Besides, when marking papers which indicate that the writers are of nearly equal merit except as to spelling, examiners will always show decided preference for pupils who possess proper knowledge of orthography.

SENIOR GRADE.—FIRST PAPER.—GIRLS.

Report of WILLIAM MAGENNIS, M.A.

The great majority of the candidates show a want of proper training in English Composition. There is no evidence of thought in their essays; and their prevailing impression seems to be that quantity instead of quality is an Intermediate examiner's criterion of merit. Fully seventy per cent. of the essays were demant—more or less incoherent—on the necessity of Love in one's life, and the platitudes and quotations pressed into this service were of the tritest kind.

The grammar papers were slightly below the average; and here again the absence of thought on the part of the candidate was conspicuous; while wonderful to relate, untidiness was equally notable, particularly in the analysis work.

The questions which called for the repetition of certain passages of "Coriolanus" were better answered than in the case of the boys; indeed so well had the text been committed to memory that in most papers there was a marked tendency to superabundant quotation.

Whereas there is a marked trace of careful and almost elaborate training in the Senior boys' papers, there is a regrettable deficiency in this respect exhibited by the papers of the Senior girls.

SENIOR GRADE.—SECOND PAPER.—GIRLS.

Report of W. MACNEILE DIXON, M.A.

The answering was accurate and full on the sections of this paper dealing with Macaulay's Essays on *Clive* and *Warren Hastings*. The geography was less satisfactory, and the literature very disappointing.

Both this year and last I was struck by the fact that the girls of the Senior Grade exhibited no greater facility in dealing with questions involving breadth of treatment, or any mental process besides memory, than the girls of the Preparatory Grade. As far as I am able to judge, there is no advance in intellectual grasp or reflective power at all proportionate to the age of the candidates. The teaching of literature in the schools of Ireland, if the results be at all faithfully reflected in the answers read by me, must be singularly mechanical and unintelligent.

MIDDLE GRADE.—FIRST PAPER.—GIRLS.

Report of Rev. HENRY EVANS, D.D.

In the choice of subjects set for composition, seven per cent. of the girls took " Life at the Equator," twenty-seven per cent. chose " The Influence of Literature on Social Life," and sixty-six per cent.

> " Absence of occupation is not rest,
> A mind quite vacant is a mind distrest."

The essays were good, many were excellent, and a few reached a still higher order of merit. Too frequently the third subject was treated as though it were equivalent to " The *Evils* of Idleness."

The answering in *grammar* was the poorest part of the work. Shortcomings in knowledge of the subject were generally evident. I feel convinced that, in the course of school operations, pains enough had not been taken in the practice of parsing fully.

As in the case of the boys, *analysis* was usually well done. The candidates have an intelligent acquaintance with the principles of this part of grammar, and show considerable aptness in their application. Judging from the answers to the question "What is a preposition?" I conclude that definitions are drawn from more uniform sources than those supplying boys' schools. Not unfrequently it was said that prepositions were used to connect words, and show the relations between the *things* which *words represent*.

After a quite sympathetic examination of the answering of the candidates, both male and female, I would fain impress on teachers the importance of framing, with the aid of the best more recent grammars, their own definitions; and sparing no pains to elucidate the terms, which advanced knowledge and highest experience have deemed the fittest, in which to present the principles and usages of English grammar. It is not to be expected that pupils generally will possess any considerable variety of books; it all the more, therefore, devolves on teachers to collect and collate the teachings of the best authors, and exhibit the results with the aid of the happiest illustrative examples. Such teaching will certainly stimulate and otherwise pay.

The answering of the girls in *Paradise Lost*, Book I., and *Lycidas* reached a high degree of merit. The passages quoted were often given as correctly and in as good order as if transcribed from the printed book.

Explanation of passages and of words used in more or less obsolete senses was creditably done. The metrical structure of Milton's verse seems to be generally understood, and by a very considerable number of candidates the scanning was performed with ease and accuracy. In the knowledge of *Prosody*, marked and most gratifying progress has been made since I last examined in Milton. But more prominence should be given to this subject still, and every endeavour put forth to cultivate and foster literary taste and judgment. The study of an English classic should be made to serve a higher end than that of being merely a medium for learning scraps of ancient geography, ancient history, mythology, and such like. These should always be subordinated to the knowledge of literature, as such—the supreme end ever being the attainment of power to appreciate literary beauty and skill in the practice of literary art.

MIDDLE GRADE.—SECOND PAPER.—GIRLS.

Report of HENRY S. MACRAN, M.A.

The answering of the girls candidates in English Literature was on the whole excellent, and far superior to that of the boys in the same grade. The same may be said of their answering in Physical Geography. On the other hand, their knowledge of History seemed to be decidedly inferior. They seemed to have understood too little, and learned too much by heart. Many of them betrayed an extraordinary ignorance of such common words as "abjure," and "allegiance."

A word might be said about the diffuseness of the girls' answers, and their waste of time and paper. To give an instance—The question was asked, " Who wrote Joseph Andrews ? What work was it intended to satirise ?" The answer to this should be given in two words. But many girls appeared to think their answer would not be complete, except they gave the dates and plots of both works, the dates of the birth and death of both authors, and an account of the effect that the publication of the satire had on their personal relations.

JUNIOR GRADE.—FIRST PAPER.—GIRLS.

Report of DANIEL CROLY, M.A.

The paper consisted of three parts: (A) Composition, (B) English Grammar, (C) Scott's Lay of the Last Minstrel, Cantos IV., V., VI. I shall deal with each part separately.

A. *Composition.* Of the subjects proposed, the second, " *Ulysses,*" was selected by a large majority of the candidates, and it was for many an unhappy selection. The study of Lamb's *Adventures of Ulysses* furnished more matter than could well be treated of in the time at their disposal, and the natural result was that hurry induced carelessness, and numbers, who I am sure would have written fairly good essays on either of the other subjects, returned pages of unpunctuated, and in too many cases, of ungrammatical sentences and clauses introduced by countless repetitions of such words as " and," " so," " then," " now," etc.   The compositions on " Animal Pets " and " Necessity is the Mother of Invention " were of the ordinary Junior Grade type, and nearly all of them, if I may judge from the general treatment of the subject, and more especially from the anecdotes quoted, were reproductions from some school works on essay writing.

B. *Grammar.* The analysis was badly done by nearly all the students, and it was evident that the subject had not received the attention it deserves. A very large number who scored high marks on the other grammar questions did not know the meaning of the term *simple sentence*, the prevailing idea seeming to be that *complex* or *compound* sentences, if easy, were the same as *simple* sentences.   The programme prescribed for the Junior Grade only " Analysis of simple sentences," and a simple sentence is defined by grammarians as one which contains not more than one subject and one predicate.

The parsing was fairly good, but there is still room for great improvement. It is not enough to tell what part of speech a word is, the relation of the word to other words in the sentence should be given. In parsing the word " that " in extract (b) of question V., viz.:—

> " Soon on the hill's steep verge he stood
> *That* looks o'er Branksome's towers and wood."

It is not sufficient to say that " that " is a relative pronoun—the answer should say what its antecedent is, and how it is connected with " looks." The correction of the faulty sentences was satisfactory, but many either omitted to give any reasons for their corrections, or gave wrong and ungrammatical ones which proved that their corrections were nothing better than lucky guesses. The answering to question IV. as to the difference between *transitive* and *intransitive* verbs was not sufficiently accurate, and a great many, though they gave a correct definition of each, quoted examples which led one to believe that the distinction was not clearly understood.

O. *Scott's Lay of the Last Minstrel* (Cantos IV., V., VI.). The
"Lay" had evidently been well and carefully prepared. As usual the
text was known by rote. I saw a great improvement in the way in which
the quotations asked were turned out, the handwriting, spelling, and
sequence being very good. There was also a marked improvement
shown in the answers to such questions as the sixth, seventh, and ninth,
which were introduced to test the intelligence rather than the memory
of the candidates. There was a tendency, however, to spin out the
answers by long quotations from the text.

JUNIOR GRADE.—SECOND PAPER.—GIRLS.

Report of J. D. COLCLOUGH.

I examined 970 papers in English (second paper, girls). The subjects
were Lamb's *Ulysses*, English and Irish History, and the Geography of
the British Isles, including Physical Geography.

In respect of Lamb's *Ulysses*, an examination of these papers would
leave upon any fair and candid mind the impression that there are
not a few of our schools in which ability to teach girls an English
Classic is by no means a strong point. One would think that in the
preparation of the work in question the pupils had, for the most part,
been left to themselves. The papers which displayed power to seize
upon the salient and integral points of a question, and to build up
this exercise of judgment into grammatical English sentences, were
considerably disproportionate in number to the majority. The ordinary
rules of grammar were in many cases set at defiance, and so small a
virtue as punctuation was almost generally ignored as beneath notice.
Certain idiosyncrasies of spelling that seem chronic were reproduced
this year. "Untill," for example, has yet to be exorcised.

The principals of many ladies' schools in this country may be respectfully reminded that to oblige their pupils to commit to memory the
primitive verbs of an English author is neither a necessary, nor a necessarily safe, passport of entrance into the author's mind and meaning;
and that to exact mnemonic mastery of an editor's notes—which, where
they are outside statements of facts, are merely statements of opinion—
is not a reliable educational process towards the habitual formation in
a pupil of opinions of her own. The mistaken policy to which I refer
attached to the answering in History a mediocre quality, which it would
otherwise have lacked. That is to say, certain and sundry small
historical handbooks were—in too many instances—learnt both by heart
and by rote.

The knowledge of Political Geography displayed by almost all the
pupils was extremely creditable, as being both accurate and full; but
the answering in Physical Geography was by no means so good.

It may not be amiss to add that at an examination in English such
matters as good grammar, correct spelling, and decent punctuation
count for something; and the written exhibition of them affords the best
criterion of efficient oral teaching.

PREPARATORY GRADE.—FIRST PAPER.—GIRLS.

Report of JOHN PARK, D.LITT.

I examined this year in English 525 girls of the Preparatory Grade in Composition, Grammar, and Selected Poems.

I had never before examined candidates of this grade, and I may say that the answering was, generally, as good as I had expected, and as regards spelling, writing, and punctuation much better than I had expected.

The prize compositions were really good, and sometimes very promising; the essays were as a rule fairly well composed, and displayed much power of expression, and often a very considerable ingenuity in adapting the incidents of familiar stories and introducing sentences that seemed to belong to other compositions; there was a good deal of exaggerated reflection and unreal experience, that often led to ludicrous inconsistencies and curious contradictions.

The answers in grammar were less satisfactory; many were wild and extremely careless, and some seemed to indicate that there are teachers who retain incorrect and antiquated rules and explanations.

The selected poems had been evidently read with interest and attention, and the notes seem to have been prepared even more carefully than the texts. There were many strange misconceptions, and few candidates gave fully and clearly, in their own words, the sense of four rather easy passages.

———

PREPARATORY GRADE.—SECOND PAPER.—GIRLS.

Report of W. M'NEILE DIXON, M.A., D. CROLY, M.A., and J. D. COLCLOUGH.

The answering to the questions on Lamb's *Ulysses*, with the exception of No. 3, was intelligent and full. Sufficient attention, however, does not seem to have been paid in the schools to the pronunciation of the proper names occurring in the text, names which it must be remembered are to be found in most English literary works. Teachers should also bear in mind that something more is expected than a minute knowledge of the subject-matter of the prescribed author, and such important considerations as English grammar and correct spelling and punctuation should not be neglected in the effort to "make up" the text-book.

The answering in English and Irish History showed evidence of careful preparation. With the exception of the question on the meaning of certain geographical terms, such as "Archipelago" and "delta," the Geography was well done, and it is satisfactory to note that proof of study of the map of Ireland was given by a large proportion of the candidates.

COMMERCIAL ENGLISH.

SENIOR GRADE.—Boys and Girls.

Report of JOHN PARK, D.LITT.

I examined this year in Commercial English 31 boys and 2 girls of the Senior Grade. I was much pleased with the amount and the quality of their work in general; the percentage of failures was smaller, and that of honours somewhat greater, than in either the Middle or the Junior Grade; but I noticed that the books prescribed were not so thoroughly mastered as they usually are in the ordinary English course.

MIDDLE GRADE.—Boys and Girls.

Report of JOHN PARK, D.LITT.

I examined this year in Commercial English 110 boys and 2 girls of the Middle Grade. I found their answering better than that in the lower grade, and exhibiting pretty much the same weaknesses. I noticed the decided advantage of prescribing, or at least suggesting, text-books, even though these did not seem to have been so carefully read as are the books in the ordinary English course.

JUNIOR GRADE.—Boys and Girls.

Report of JOHN PARK, D.LITT.

I examined this year in Commercial English 323 boys and 9 girls of the Junior Grade. I report that there is a very decided improvement on last year's bad answering as regards writing, spelling, neatness, information, and intelligence.

The copying exercise was often very creditable.

The Geography was better prepared than the History. Many candidates were deplorably ignorant of the ordinary as well as of the commercial history of the prescribed period; they confounded, *ex. gr.*, the Industrial revolution at the end of last century with the French Revolution of the same date, or with the Revolution of 1688—and their wild guesses often betrayed an amusing and amazing misapprehension of the simplest economic facts.

PRÉCIS WRITING.

MIDDLE GRADE.—Boys and Girls.

Report of A. J. NICOLLS, LL.B.

I examined the Précis Writing of the Middle Grade pupils this year. Last year I reported defective teaching, and consequent poor quality of the work submitted to me in this part of the Intermediate course. I am glad to be able to report that general and decided improvement is apparent in the Précis work submitted this year.

Précis writing being of importance in the Civil Service and in many high-class mercantile offices, it is satisfactory to find that it is receiving a fair share of attention in some of the well-managed Intermediate schools.

FRENCH.

Senior Grade.—Boys.

Report of Georges E. Barrier.

A.

The weak point is the Grammar and Composition. There can be no doubt that the answering in both these divisions ought to be much better than it is, and I do not consider that they offered this year more difficulty than in former years. If the composition is not satisfactory, the apparent reason is that less time has been devoted to it than to the text-books. In the Grammar, question No. 2 on the formation of the suffix *ment* in French adverbs, question No. 5 on diminutives, and question No. 6 on the subjunctive, were indifferently answered. As regards question No. 8, some candidates answered in a manner which suggested that the teacher had gone over that ground with the pupil, but the latter had failed to understand. As regards questions 2 and 5, I may be permitted to say that the study of a modern tongue—for senior students especially—should not comprise the rules of syntax only, but also a few important rules bearing on the formation of words, on the relation existing between certain usual French forms and the Latin forms from which they are derived. This is not asking too much, when, as in the present instance, the questions are set on general lines, and have a general importance as suggesting interesting examples of word-formation from the mother tongue.

The prescribed works of Lamartine and Corneille were both well prepared, but more pains seem to have been bestowed on the former. The translation from the uniform French verse was often stiff and too literal. On the other hand, the Examiner has pleasure to say that some of the translations from *le Tailleur* were admirable, showing as they did a thorough grasp of the text and a great and facile command over the English tongue.

In the translation at sight, the poetry was found easier than the prose. As in the case of *le Tailleur*, some students, who stand high all round, did great credit to themselves.

To sum up, I would say that the answering is acceptable and creditable in most parts, but that the answering in the first part, comprising Grammar and Composition, is scarcely worthy of Senior Grade students.

B

To remedy the weak state of the Composition I would suggest that more time be devoted to it. It will be in the interest of both the teachers and students if such composition be graduated as to difficulty. Better and safer results are attained by graduating the Composition, removing difficulties at the outset, than by selecting for translation pieces at random from authors whose prose, entangled and unconcise at times, cannot be considered a safe ground for useful exercise.

Middle Grade.—Boys.

Report of F. J. Amours.

The results of this paper are very fair, and compare favourably with my previous experiences of Middle Grade boys. It is true that the failures amount to about a third, but the candidates that have passed have reached a high percentage, and over forty per cent. have attained honour marks. The answers to grammatical questions are more successful than the translation of idioms. Middle Grade candidates should not lose sight entirely of what they have learned in previous years, and I was surprised to see how many were unable to translate the numeral adjectives *third* and *fourth.* The handwriting seems to be deteriorating; on the other hand the English spelling has improved, if we leave the failures out of account. The 'over-age' papers are very weak.

JUNIOR GRADE—BOYS.

Report of Rev. J. F. HOGAN, A. COGERY, and VICTOR OGER.

We found the work done by the Junior Grade boys, on the whole, very fair. The answers to the grammar questions were in most cases satisfactory, and there were fewer omissions than in previous years: the books set had been well prepared, and the translations from them were generally accurate, in many cases very good indeed; whilst the unseen piece of French prose was unusually well done by a large proportion of the boys. We cannot however find much evidence of training in the construction of French sentences in any but very few papers; nine-tenths of the attempts submitted to us were lamentably poor, and we cannot too thoroughly insist upon the necessity for teachers in all grades to give their best attention to this part of the work *from the beginning.* Many of the papers gave proofs of a good deal of study of the language, and yet of ignorance of its use in the commonest grammatical and idiomatic constructions; the boys' future progress must prove much more difficult than it need be if they had practised composition earlier.

As regards the over-age boys, very few of them treated the examination seriously; many sent in almost blank answer books, and scarcely any of them showed any knowledge at all of either words or grammar.

PREPARATORY GRADE.—BOYS.

Report of GEORGE E. BARRIER AND FREDERIC SPENCER, M.A.

The grammar questions were, for the most part, very satisfactorily answered. A strangely large number of boys failed however to give correctly the present subjunctive of *croir,* and the masculine of *tout,* although this latter occurred in one of the passages set for translation.

The composition was much less satisfactory than the grammar, a considerable number of versions being practically valueless. Indeed, it is clear that much greater practice in this part of the work is urgently needed. On the other hand, many candidates gave evidence of good work and careful teaching; and it was by no means easy to select from among a number of excellent papers those which should be recommended for composition prizes.

In prepared translation a very large number of generally correct versions were sent up.

The unprepared translation was exceedingly well done by a small minority of the candidates; but a considerable proportion failed altogether to grasp the general sense of the passage set.

A deplorably large number of papers exhibited gross ignorance of English grammar and orthography. Frequent blunders were made in the spelling of the commonest and shortest English words; and words of ordinary occurrence, containing two or three syllables, were spelt in an astonishing variety of ways. The correct orthography of *kitchen* was indeed almost the exception. Expressions such as "all them flowers," "it never asked for nothing," "why has you come?" were of very frequent occurrence.

Some of the answer books exhibited much slovenliness and general carelessness. In the case of many boys the answers were not numbered. Others crowded several answers into one page, or scattered the fragments of one answer promiscuously among the others. Many boys, again, wrote out whole tenses where only a single person was asked for; several attempted to conjugate the word *preterite* in answer to a question designed to elicit the "preterite of *manger*." Others failed to observe that the more difficult points in composition were elucidated in footnotes. We would earnestly recommend teachers to provide young students with some preliminary training in the art of answering a paper in intelligent and orderly style.

From the constant admixture of Latin, Italian, and German words, even in the papers of well prepared candidates, we fear that certain boys may be taking up more subjects than they can efficiently pursue at such an early age. In the case of such young students, teachers would do well to encourage intensive rather than extensive work.

There were many indications that the set books are prepared by a certain proportion of candidates in a most mechanical and unintelligent way; and this with the tacit, if not the expressed, approval of responsible teachers. It is indeed hardly possible to imagine anything more mischievous than the kind of training which has led up to some of the phenomena observed in this year's papers. In some cases an almost faultless translation was preceded or followed by the translation of several lines occurring in the original context, but not forming part of the passage set. And, in one case, an excellent translation was offered of an entire *fable* of Florian, no part of which appeared in the paper of questions. It was further clear that very many boys did not even understand what they had so faithfully committed to memory.

SENIOR GRADE—GIRLS

Report of P. J. AMOURS.

The Senior Grade girls have acquitted themselves most creditably, over sixty per cent. of the candidates obtaining honours, and the failures being very few. The composition deserves a special word of praise. The set books also have been read with care, Lamartine especially. The unseen passage from Taine was not without its difficulties; but they have been successfully overcome by a great number of the candidates, a very fair number of whom give a clever translation of the picturesque phraseology of the original.

MIDDLE GRADE.—GIRLS.

Report of F. J. AMOUR.

The only remark I have to make about this portion of the Middle Grade is that the girls have done better than the boys, except in the unseen prose passage. A description of Vendean warfare should have offered few difficulties after a study of "Derrière les Haies"; however the extract was found rather stiff by a majority of the pupils, and excellent renderings are scarce among the girls than among the boys.

JUNIOR GRADE.—GIRLS.

Report of ELPHEGE JANAU.

I have examined the papers of the girls, Junior Grade, and the result is on the whole creditable to both teachers and pupils.

In *Grammar* the answers to questions one and two on the plural and feminine were generally good.—Very few, however, could give the masculine of "tranquille" or the plural of "un bel arbre." Question four was answered fairly well. More attention ought to be given to the numbers. Question five showed in many a very imperfect knowledge of the irregular verbs and a want of method in answering, a whole tense being sometimes given when only two persons were required. The really weak point in the grammar was shown by questions three and six. Few candidates had grasped the proper use of the relative and interrogative pronouns, or the difference between "cela" and "celui-là" which **were** frequently given as the French corresponding to the adjectival forms "this" and "that," as for instance: cela cheval, this horse; celui-là livre, that book. The participles will require a great deal of attention from the teachers. Many of the candidates had not the remotest idea of what was required. Even the words active, passive, and neuter verbs were apparently not understood.

The *Composition* was on the **whole** fair; many candidates showed intelligence and care, though often coupled with very imperfect knowledge. In several cases the work was highly creditable.

The *Translation* from the prepared books was good, though the French construction was often followed too closely. In some papers there was hardly any fault to find. On the other hand there were a few cases where it was impossible to discover in the English any trace of the original French, the candidate's imagination being evidently as fertile as her knowledge was scanty.

A curious want of thought was exhibited in the dates of Joan of Arc's birth and death. According to a good many candidates, the length of her life varied between five years and two hundred, while a few actually placed the date of her death many years previous to that of her birth.

The unprepared translation was satisfactory.

The want of order so often complained of must again be mentioned. Questions are taken in small fragments, which are scattered here and there among other questions. If only teachers and students realised the trouble of collecting those fragments so that each question may be marked separately, and also the possibility of some part of their answers being unmarked, I feel certain this complaint would not have to be repeated. The candidate could easily leave a blank space sufficient for the answer, and fill it in when convenient. In this way the work would look better, and much trouble would be avoided.

PREPARATORY GRADE.—GIRLS.

Report of Rev. J. F. HOGAN.

The papers of the Preparatory Grade (Girls) examined by me this year were, in many respects, satisfactory. They showed careful preparation and close attention to the rules of composition as well as to those of grammar. Indeed, it would be difficult to expect more from candidates so young, who have a long course before them. It is curious that the department in which the Junior Grade boys most excelled—namely, the rendering of the piece for translation at sight, was the one in which the Preparatory Grade girls were most deficient. The attempts at the translation of a very simple passage were almost ridiculous even in the case of girls who scored high marks otherwise.

The prepared passages and the questions in grammar were well done, and several of the sentences given for translation into French were very correctly rendered.

SENIOR GRADE.—COMMERCIAL PAPER.

Report of G. E. BARBIER.

The passages from French into English were well done on the whole, some of the papers showing to great advantage both as to the correct rendering of the commercial terms and the idiomatic turn of the translation. The rendering into French, however, was not satisfactory. It is evident that this part of the programme has not been so carefully attended to as the other. Besides the general weakness of the composition, the vocabulary which would be required to do justice to it was inadequate and inaccurate.

I, therefore, recommend that more time should be devoted to the vocabulary of articles that are bought and sold, and to the composition.

MIDDLE GRADE.—COMMERCIAL PAPER.

Report of F. J. AMOUTE.

The second half of this paper has been fairly well done, but the translation of the English phrases and of the letter was very unsatisfactory. Out of ninety-eight candidates, thirty-nine failed to gain any marks at all, thirty-five were under twenty-five per cent., and eight only succeeded in obtaining over fifty per cent. Yet almost all the expressions to be translated were of an elementary character, and I was lenient in my marking.

JUNIOR GRADE.—COMMERCIAL PAPER.

Report of VICTOR OGER.

About 350 boys sent in answers to the Junior Commercial Paper (French): 8 left hardly anything to be desired; 51 were good, and 102 very fair; the rest almost worthless, 11 indeed simply nil.

Of 16 boys over-age, 3 answered well, and three others fairly, none of the other papers had any practical value.

Eight junior girls also took up the Commercial Paper; two of them did excellently in almost every part of it; the others, with one or two exceptions, made very satisfactory attempts, though none of them gained one-half of the marks obtained by the best candidate.

Judging the work as a whole, I found it more promising than I expected, and in many instances superior to that examined by me this year, and previously, both from English and Scotch schools presenting pupils of either sex and of about the same age. I regret to add that in almost all the papers I found the mere *word-knowledge* (" vocabulary") more deficient than the construction of *sentences from or into* French.

GERMAN,

GENERAL REMARKS.

Report of V. STEINBERGER, M.A.

The study of German has, as the rapidly increasing numbers of candidates testify, taken a firm hold in the Irish schools. This year, for the first time, the Answer Books sent in amount to more than one thousand. With this increase in numbers the excellence of work has kept pace. There is a fairly large number of candidates, especially in the Preparatory and Junior Grades, who promise well. The great drawback in these two grades is the want of method. Not unfrequently one meets one half of an answer separated from the other half by several pages. A careful answering of test papers during the year of preparation might cure this defect.

The word for word translation is given by many in a very confused manner. The candidates do not seem to read or understand the directions given for this purpose. I would suggest that they should write this part of translation in two columns—in the one the English words and in the other corresponding foreign ones.

SENIOR GRADE.—BOYS AND GIRLS.

Report of V. STEINBERGER.

The grammar questions, with the exception of questions one and three, were well answered.

The composition however, especially that of the boys, was very middling indeed. It would seem, as pointed out in the Middle Grade, that sufficient time and care are not devoted to this most important branch of the language in which no real progress can be made except by continuous and regular exercises. A few sentences translated carefully every day during the scholastic year would enable a candidate to face any moderate piece of composition creditably, and give him an extensive knowledge of advanced grammar that would facilitate the rest of his work immensely.

The majority of the candidates did not see the reason of the inversion in the prescribed passage B in the lines :—

> Stürzt die Lawin' einmal ;
> Fuhr erst der Schnee zu Thal,

and missed consequently the meaning of the first four lines. The remainder of the prescribed passages was well rendered.

The translation at sight, especially of the passage of poetry, was done satisfactorily.

MIDDLE GRADE.—BOYS AND GIRLS.

Report of V. STEINBERGER, M.A.

The answering in grammar was good; but the knowledge of grammar did not keep pace with the progress in composition. There was, with a few notable exceptions, a decided want of a fairly stocked vocabulary perceptible throughout; such ordinary words as "to wait for," "to seem," "to complete," "to pass (time)," etc., were unknown to many. Candidates in the Middle Grade are expected to know the difference of meaning of verbs like scheinen and erscheinen, and the construction of verbs like warten and erwarten. My impression is that too little time is devoted to composition in which progress is only possible by continuous practice.

The translation of the prescribed passages was fair. The rendering of the translation at sight on the whole satisfactory.

JUNIOR GRADE.—BOYS AND GIRLS.

Report of V. STEINBERGER, M.A.

The answering in grammar was creditable except in the questions on the declension of the comparatives of adjectives and on the conjugation of regular verbs. Whilst the irregular verbs seemed to be well known, indeed, the regular verb "zeigen" was mistaken either for "ziehen," or appeared twisted into other fantastic forms. The same weakness manifested itself in the conjugation in the past tense of the verb "sich erinnern." More exercises in conjugating verbs in all their tenses and moods will remedy this defect.

The colloquial phrases of the composition were rendered well on the average. In the continuous piece of composition I remarked, besides the numerous mistakes in construction, especially a non-observance of the rules of the declension of adjectives ; even candidates who showed by their answers in the grammar part a thorough knowledge in declining adjectives, failed to utilise their knowledge in the composition. Want of sufficient exercise in composition when preparing for their work is the cause of these mistakes. Another striking feature was the very frequent translation of "everything" by "etwas."

The book prescribed for translation was carefully studied, as the answers to the questions attached to the passages showed. The rendering of the translation at sight showed a considerably greater advance and vocabulary than the Preparatory Grade.

PREPARATORY GRADE.—BOYS AND GIRLS.

Report of V. STEINBERGER, M.A.

The weakness in the declensions of nouns and adjectives pointed out in my last year's report has almost entirely disappeared. Even the weaker candidates made a good attempt in answering the question given to test this part of grammar. Fair knowledge was exhibited in the prepositions and verbs. Many missed the question on the numerals, because they did not appear to know the distinction between ordinal and cardinal numbers. Only a couple were able to answer the question on the use of zu and a. More attention should be paid to the few general rules on German orthography.

The composition, considering the age of the candidates, was promising on the average. A very frequent mistake was owing to the circumstance that they construed the verb sein with an accusative, e.g., "Frederick said that he was their duke" was generally translated by: "Friedrich sagte, dass er ihren Herzog wäre," instead of "Ihr Herzog."

A number of candidates broke down in the second part of the prescribed translation. They seem not to have read the whole book prescribed for this grade. Several failures are due to this cause. Few knew where the Thuringerwald was situated.

The translation of the unprescribed passage was middling. Many lost the thread of the latter half on account of not construing well.

A few candidates seemed to have been prevented from finishing their paper, because they were yet too unfamiliar with German handwriting.

COMMERCIAL GERMAN.

JUNIOR, MIDDLE, AND SENIOR GRADES.—BOYS AND GIRLS.

Report of V. STEINBERGER, M.A.

A considerable improvement is perceptible in the answering compared with that of last year. The vocabulary of the candidates seemed to be better stocked with commercial expressions and phrases. In every one of the three grades, especially in the Senior, very fair answers were given.

ITALIAN.

Senior Grade.—Boys.

Report of A. Farinelli.

Twenty-one boys presented for examination in this Grade, and I am very glad to state that the compositions of almost all have been fairly done. The answering of the Grammar questions was very good, the translations excellent, and, except three, all passed with Honours. Only one failed.

Senior Grade.—Girls.

Report of A. Farinelli.

The few Senior girls, 8, were not inferior to the boys; none failed, and, except one, all got high Honours.

Middle Grade.—Boys.

Report of A. Farinelli.

This Grade gave in Composition comparatively a much better result than the two lower Grades, but in Grammar I have found among the candidates scarcely one who could explain clearly the difference between the Italian gerund and the present participle. However, the rest of the work was sufficiently well done.

Middle Grade.—Girls.

Report of A. Farinelli.

For the girls of this Grade we have nothing to add to what we have said about the boys of the same Grade, as the results of both were almost equal.

Junior Grade.—Boys.

Report of A. Farinelli.

The number of the boys of this Grade, 113, was the greatest, and larger than in the last year, but I regret to state that they have not given proof of having studied very much, as 25 candidates obtained no marks in Composition, and the answering in Grammar was generally not good; however, the prescribed and unprescribed passages were translated tolerably well.

Junior Grade.—Girls.

Report of A. Farinelli.

These girls were inferior in Composition to the boys of the same Grade but somewhat superior in Grammar: their translations into English were rather satisfactory, and the failures in the same proportion as among the boys.

Preparatory Grade.—Boys.

Report of A. Farinelli.

I have examined 62 boys of this Grade and I have found that the results in Composition were very unsatisfactory, as only four reached two-thirds of the marks assigned to it. Also, in the Grammar questions they have given no proof of a good preparation. The translation of the prepared passage, however, was rather creditable, but not so that of the passage at sight.

Preparatory Grade.—Girls.

Report of A. Farinelli.

I am sorry to report that the few Preparatory Grade girls were in general inferior to the boys, chiefly in Composition, in which six got no marks at all.

Middle and Senior Grades.—Commercial Paper.—Boys.

Report of A. Farinelli.

I have to report that this time only three candidates presented themselves for examination in Commercial Italian; one Middle Grade candidate who failed, and two Senior Grade who succeeded very well.

Comparing the present examination with that of the last year, I find that the whole number of the candidates is increased by almost a hundred. I have also remarked in the Middle and Senior Grades some progress in writing Italian, but not in the other two grades.

SPANISH.

Middle Grade.—Boys.

Report of V. Steinberger, M.A.

Of the few candidates that presented themselves only one gave proof of careful preparation. His answering in Grammar, Composition and Translation was very good.

CELTIC.

ALL GRADES.—BOYS.

Report of Rev. J. E. H. MURPHY, M.A.

(a.) The answering in all Grades was, on the whole, good; and, considering that the examination papers were a little more difficult this year than last year, the results were very satisfactory.

In the Preparatory and Junior Grades many presented themselves for examination who had not made any serious study of the course: some having relied on translations got by rote, but not knowing, when the test came, where to begin or where to end; two of them giving a translation which had nothing in common with the passage of which it purported to be a translation; others failing to give the "word for word" translation, but supplying other translations "on chance." This kind of preparation is worse than useless, and received the reward which was meet. The candidates who failed, in this way, in translating, were lamentably weak in grammar and composition.

The compositions in all Grades (with the exceptions just mentioned) were good; and some of them even excellent.

(b.) The matters needing special attention in preparing students, seem still to be the declension of irregular nouns, the comparison of irregular adjectives, the conjugation of irregular verbs, the study of idiomatic phrases, and the proper collocation of the various classes of words in forming compound sentences.

Proper attention has not been given to accuracy of translation in the Middle and Senior Grades.

ALL GRADES.—GIRLS.

Report of Rev. J. E. H. MURPHY, M.A.

Four candidates presented themselves for examination—one in each Grade. Of these three obtained passes with Honours, and one a pass without Honours. The answering of the candidate in the Junior Grade was very good, and her composition was excellent.

DOMESTIC ECONOMY.

SENIOR GRADE.—GIRLS ONLY.

Report of MARY BELLINGHAM TODD.

The answering of the Seniors in Domestic Economy was decidedly good.

In very few cases were the answers wanting in originality, while, at the same time, they afforded ample proof that the text-books had not been neglected.

Where knowledge of the actual practical work was required in the answer, it was frequently supplemented with an intelligent "reason why."

The average work of the average students was excellent.

The failing noticeable in many of the answers was a want of conciseness, as if the students were answering a number of questions instead of one. With this exception the work is encouraging, and must have an important bearing upon the home life.

MIDDLE GRADE—GIRLS ONLY.

Report of FANNIE GALLAHER.

The answers of this grade this year were uniformly intelligent, and afforded indisputable proof that the general education of the candidates was advancing steadily if not rapidly. The questions which required specific knowledge of the subject were not so successfully answered, on the whole, as those which gave scope to a display of that liberal learning now so popular with educationists. There was less of the home-girl and more of the world-woman in the answers—less practical information and more theoretical deduction. The demands of the age do not allow such a state of affairs to be any cause for regret; but, at the same time, the ordinary examiner cannot be reproached for hoping that the day may come when the girls of Ireland will recognise the fact that higher education, like certain proverbial chickens and other things less innocent, must come home to roost. Absolute, positive knowledge of the laws of life, home and market, will ever be a potent factor in our everyday happiness, and until this truth is grasped in a sensible fashion, the tendency of the class-room will be towards the development of the student at the expense of the woman, rather than of the woman and the student, *pari passu.*

In my opinion it would be very advisable if a system of object lessons in Domestic Economy could be devised and put into operation in every school worthy of the name where boarders are taken. Practice will always teach better than precept, let the study be what it may, and it would be almost as fair to expect pianoforte playing from a girl whose idea of music was based and built on Bookstro, as to look for housekeeping from one who had never stirred a saucepan nor dusted out a sitting room. The attempts at cookery given in some of the answers were enough to produce mental dyspepsia.

May I suggest to teachers that it would save a great deal of time and trouble if pupils were made to understand that there is little use in the elaborate verbal arrangements they sometimes make to conceal their want of definite knowledge? There are few examiners who were born yesterday; and those who were born many years ago can see at a glance through the little plots occasionally woven for the purpose of winning marks without earning them.

JUNIOR GRADE—GIRLS ONLY.

Report of FANNIE GALLAHER and MARY BELLINGHAM TODD.

Our opinion respecting the answering of the Juniors in Domestic Economy is that it was on the whole satisfactory.

In the case of some students the work was not only creditably done as a lesson, but was apparently the result of a pleasant study, intelligently guided, beyond the region of mere book work.

On the other hand some answers clearly indicated a want of definite knowledge in the elementary branches, such as the meaning of "organ," "structure," or "function." Closely allied to absurdity were some of the answers on "How to roast a sirloin of beef?" Nearly half the students recommended the meat to be held close to the fire for a few minutes before putting it into the oven; and again not a few regulated the heat of the body by means of a thermometer.

It would be an advantage if the students during school lessons were obliged to keep to the point in answering questions in order to avoid misapprehension as to the nature of questions:—*e.g.,* in very few cases was an intelligent description of a working-man's cottage given; it was usually a long composition on the furniture of the cottage or the habits and possibilities of the workman and his family.

ELEMENTARY MECHANICS.

Senior Grade.—Boys only.

Report of James C. Rea, b.a.

The answering in this subject was on the whole satisfactory. Of the 101 examined—including 10 over-age—70 passed and 31 failed. Of those that passed, 28 passed with honours, and a few got nearly full marks.

I met some cases in which I suspected an unintelligent use of formulæ.

Questions 4, 7, 8, and 12 were, in general, badly answered; but I was pleased to find such an accurate grasp of fundamental principles evinced by those candidates who worked 7, 8, and 12, correctly.

It is surprising the number who failed to do Question 6, from not knowing how to find the volume of a cylinder. In the case of Senior Boys such ignorance of the elements of Mensuration, at a time when they are about to leave school, is inexcusable.

Many who answered the latter part of Question 5 were unable to give an accurate definition of acceleration, and very few could tell how a force is measured dynamically.

PLANE TRIGONOMETRY.

Senior Grade.—Boys and Girls.

Report of Rev. Francis Lennon, d.d.

The answering in Trigonometry of both boys and girls has been extremely good. Not merely is the percentage of passes high, but the general quality of the answering is excellent; and although only one boy has obtained full marks, a large proportion of those who have qualified have shown remarkable skill in the manipulation of trigonometrical formulæ.

ALGEBRA AND ARITHMETIC.

SENIOR GRADE.—BOYS AND GIRLS.

Report of M. W. JOSEPH FRY, M.A.

The answering of the boys in the Senior Grade was satisfactory.

Failures resulted more from inaccuracy of work than from ignorance of theory. This was particularly exemplified in the attempts to obtain the coefficient of a power of x in a binomial expansion; a very large number of candidates after giving the coefficient right in its undeveloped form failed to approximate even to the final result.

Question No. 8 was answered well by a considerable number of boys. Many boys who showed that they had enough theoretical knowledge to do question No. 9 did not go on with their work.

The simultaneous equations were not answered well, impossible answers were shown up to No. 12 in a great number of cases, and no attempts were made to verify answers which admitted of easy verification.

All the questions, with the exception perhaps of a part of No. 10, were answered by the Senior Grade boys.

The Senior Grade girls worked somewhat more **correctly than the** boys, but their answering was of an inferior type.

EUCLID.

SENIOR GRADE.—BOYS AND GIRLS.

Report of W. M'F. ORR, M.A.

The proportion of failures was small, the propositions, especially those of the first four books, being well done by most of the students. Many candidates however did not treat the doctrine of proportion in any consistent logical method. The fifth question was badly answered, and only a few candidates stated the definition of proportion in such words as showed clearly that they understood it. In the seventh question many candidates, while giving Euclid's definition of duplicate ratio, proved that similar figures are to each other as the squares on their homologous sides instead of the theorem set; their answers were thus not consistent. In doing the eighth question many did not confine themselves to what is usually considered Euclid, but used Algebra also. In both the seventh and eighth questions many considered the statement that when three straight lines are proportional, the first is to the last as the square on the first is to the square on the second, as being not the enunciation of a theorem but a definition.

Few candidates did deductions. The answers to the eleventh question were noteworthy from their large number and general badness; the attempts made to deduce the result from the corresponding theorem for a line divided into two parts being, with scarcely an exception, extremely illogical.

MIDDLE GRADE—BOYS.

Report of C. J. JOLY, M.A.

I have little to add to former reports on this subject. The answering as a rule was very good, and the candidates appear to have been well taught.

I must, however, again refer to the needless repetition of enunciations and of data in comparing triangles. Students seem to think this is necessary, and they consequently lose much valuable time. In some cases students apologized for using symbols. Had they read the note on the paper they would have seen that apology was unnecessary, but it is generally necessary that the symbols used should be commonly accepted or carefully defined. I have no objection to the use of $(BD \cdot DC)^2$ for $BD^2 + DC^2$, provided I can clearly see what the student means by it—a matter of considerable difficulty; but I have a decided objection to the statement $BO + OA = EF + FD$ in comparing triangles, for I can never be sure of the geometrical property desired to be expressed.

References were plentifully given, but a little discrimination in this respect is advisable. For instance, in the sixth question a reference to I. Post. 1 or 3 is not so important as a reference to III. Prop. 3, or III. Prop. 18.

In conclusion I would recommend students to read the questions before attempting them. Even some who answered brilliantly proved one proposition instead of another.

MIDDLE GRADE—GIRLS.

Report of J. P. JOHNSTON, M.A.

The answering in this Grade, as a whole, cannot be considered satisfactory. The work of many of the candidates, while exhibiting considerable familiarity with the text of Euclid, showed that their knowledge of Geometry was small. There was a large amount of bad reasoning, and essential portions of proofs were often omitted, a fault particularly noticeable in the answers to questions 1 and 8. The number of instances in which propositions different from those asked were proved, was very great.

Some of the candidates did the propositions very well, and a few did some of the deductions.

JUNIOR GRADE—BOYS OF THE PRESCRIBED AGE.

Report of J. P. JOHNSTON, M.A., PATRICK KELLY, and W. M'F. ORR, M.A.

The propositions were on the whole well done, the most noticeable defect being that where there were two sums, a very large number of students contented themselves with doing only one. In some instances they were cumbrously written out, with frequent repetitions, which involved a fruitless expenditure of time on the part of the candidates. Conjunctions were frequently misused. In many instances "and" was used instead of "therefore," leaving it doubtful whether the succeeding sentence should be regarded as an inference or an independent statement. The diagrams were frequently ill-drawn, and illegibly lettered, causing doubt and hesitation to the Examiners as to the merit of the solutions.

The treatment of the deductions by many students was highly creditable, not only on the ground of correctness, but also by reason of the geometrical knowledge and talent displayed.

The Examiners, however, regret to have to state that a considerable number who did the propositions well, passed over the deductions without making any effort to solve them; while the attempts of others consisted of purposeless constructions, unwarranted assumptions, and of a series of groundless inferences which appeared to themselves to establish the required conclusion, or to furnish the necessary construction. These attempts showed not only utter ignorance of analysis, but also of geometrical reasoning.

The Examiners would wish to call the attention of teachers to the great importance of the cultivation of analysis, which appears to be considerably neglected.

JUNIOR GRADE.—GIRLS.

Report of PATRICK KELLY.

The answering in this grade, when taken as a whole, can hardly be regarded as satisfactory, there being a large proportion of failures. Many candidates appear to have presented themselves in this subject without any serious preparation. In a great number of instances, long and comparatively difficult propositions, such as No. 8, were correctly written out by candidates who not only missed simple propositions, but made mistakes in attempting them, which would go to show that they had very confused conceptions of first principles. This inequality of answering made it difficult for the Examiner to resist the frequently-recurring suspicion that some propositions had been learned partly by rote, and reproduced without being clearly understood. In propositions having more than one case, the first only was, as a rule, given, with an equivalent loss of marks.

Of those who have passed, many have sent in excellent papers, not only proving the propositions with accuracy and intelligence, but in some cases attempting the deductions with success, and with a degree of elegance which showed skilful training and considerable originality. The mechanical part of the work was everything that could be desired—legible writing, neat figures distinctly lettered, and a very lucid disposition of the work on paper.

I would respectfully suggest that more attention ought to be paid to this subject; and that teachers should use the most searching tests to ascertain whether or not propositions, even when faultlessly written out, are thoroughly understood, as girls appear to have very quick memories, which enable them to furnish correct solutions with but little aid from the understanding.

JUNIOR GRADE.—BOYS—OVER-AGE.

Report of O. J. JOLY, M.A.

The answering on this paper cannot be regarded as very satisfactory. Question No. 9 was perhaps more generally and more fully answered than any of the others, even by those who had shown a very imperfect knowledge of the properties of a parallelogram in question No. 8. Many students who gave a proof that two circles cannot touch in two points, applied it only to internal contact, and went on to an incorrect proof for external contact. There was also large confusion of the terms "touching" and "cutting." In No. 7 the case in which the segment is greater than a semi-circle was frequently given, and No. 8 was also well done. A good deal of pure carelessness was evident in No. 4, the equality of the various parallelograms being shown, while the addition was incorrectly done.

PREPARATORY GRADE.—BOYS.

Report of THOMAS W. INWOOD, M.A., and Rev. THOMAS POWER.

The results of the examination in Euclid in the Preparatory Grade (Boys) are decidedly satisfactory. The papers have been done really well by the majority of the candidates, and the failures are comparatively few. As a rule, the work was written out neatly, and the diagrams were drawn carefully. Some few of the boys, however, were totally unprepared in the subject, and did not succeed in getting a single mark. In several cases marks were lost because some question was misread and a different proposition given from the one asked. In answering question 7 a great many omitted to state that the parallelogram described at the beginning should be a rectangle. Of the deductions, question 10 was the one which was successfully answered most frequently, while question 9, which was very easy, was seldom properly interpreted.

PREPARATORY GRADE.—GIRLS.

Report of Rev. THOMAS R. POWER.

I consider the results of the examination satisfactory. Over 66 per cent. of those examined have passed, and again over 66 per cent. of those who passed have gained honour marks. The percentages would have been still better if many girls had not misread some of the questions proposed and answered totally different ones. But in general a very creditable knowledge of the text of Euclid was exhibited, and many put their work on paper very neatly.

ALGEBRA.

MIDDLE GRADE—BOYS.

Report of SWIFT P. JOHNSTON, M.A.

The answering of the boys of the Middle Grade was most satisfactory.

One of the pleasing features in the performance of this class was the large proportion of marks obtained for the solution of problems. It is in dealing with problems that the best test is found for distinguishing between a knowledge of the principles of algebra and the mere exercise of memory in applying rules—for distinguishing true teaching from cramming. The class is therefore deserving of special praise for its success in this direction. In particular, the most difficult problem on the paper, difficult not in the solution but in the construction of the equations involved, was solved by several candidates with a completeness and "style" that would reflect credit on a much more advanced grade of mathematical knowledge.

The faults most strongly marked were carelessness and want of neatness. The loss through mere carelessness must have reached a high percentage. Perhaps the blame does not rest wholly with the students; one cannot but think that a very slight amount of instruction and practice in the proper way to write out examination answers, would have been effective to stop this leakage of marks.

MIDDLE GRADE.—GIRLS.

Report of SWIFT P. JOHNSTON, M.A.

It is perhaps a little unfortunate that, in examining the answering of the girls in this subject, the contrast with the boys was continually suggesting itself. The contrast was not in favour of the girls.

There is one point in which the girls have a decided advantage—that is in neatness. But even in their strong point there is a weakness. Neatness was too often secured at the loss of time. Duplicate working of results in the rough and in the finished form seemed the nearly universal rule. Very frequently the copy marked "rough work" was just as presentable as that which was intended for the Examiner's eye. It is true that time is not a vital element when three hours are assigned to a paper of twelve questions, nevertheless it is a factor whose importance increases as the student advances.

JUNIOR GRADE.—BOYS OF THE PRESCRIBED AGE.

Report of M. W. JOSEPH FAY, M.A., H. C. McWEENEY, M.A., and JAMES C. REA, B.A.

The examiners consider that the answering in this subject has been fair. Some candidates obtained full marks, and the work of many was done in a style which showed very careful teaching and preparation. Examining the questions in detail we find that those on simplification, Lowest Common Multiple, and the simple equations in one unknown, were in general well done. A large proportion failed at the question on Highest Common Factor, and the a factor was almost invariably omitted in the answer. The simultaneous equations were poorly done; many gave the values of x and y in terms of y and x respectively. Comparatively few attempted the problems, and except in a small number of cases the methods were defective, no clear statement being made as to what the symbols stood for.

JUNIOR GRADE.—BOYS—OVER-AGE.

Report of SWIFT P. JOHNSTON, M.A.

The answering of this class shows it to have attained a very fair standard of mathematical knowledge. There were a number of complete failures; but, on the other hand, some candidates showed such proficiency as caused surprise at finding them ranked as Over-age Juniors. Had they been required to answer the paper set in the Middle Grade, they would, no doubt, have done themselves credit.

JUNIOR GRADE.—GIRLS.

Report of Rev. FRANCIS LENNON, D.D.

In the girls' Junior Grade Algebra, a great improvement has taken place in the answering as compared with that of three years ago, when I last examined in the subject. About sixty per cent. have passed, and many of these show a good working-knowledge of the elementary rules and processes of Algebra.

PREPARATORY GRADE.—BOYS.

Report of GERALD GRIFFIN and H. C. M'WEENEY, M.A.

The answering, on the whole, was good. The candidates showed a fair knowledge of the simple rules and of the methods of finding the Highest Common Factor. The simplification questions were not so well understood, and many students appeared to be unable to deal with brackets. The question on Lowest Common Multiple was not well answered. We are of opinion that greater familiarity with the simpler cases of factors is desirable.

PREPARATORY GRADE.—GIRLS.

Report of Rev. FRANCIS LENNON, D.D.

The girls of the Preparatory Grade have answered well in Algebra. The percentage of passes is fairly high, and a large number show that they have been well trained in simplifying complicated algebraical expressions.

ARITHMETIC.

MIDDLE GRADE.—BOYS.

Report of P. A. E. DOWLING, B.A.

The answering on this paper was, on the whole, satisfactory. Only 23 per cent. failed to pass, and 42 per cent. passed with honours.

The majority of the students missed Questions 6 and 11, especially the latter, which they did not seem to consider at all carefully, as—of those who attempted it—at least 60 per cent. gave us the solution :— " There is no per-centage gain or loss on the transaction."

In many cases the solutions presented were long and the details very inaccurate though several papers were perfect models and showed complete grasp of the subject and most judicious preparation in it.

MIDDLE GRADE.—GIRLS.

Report of Rev. JAMES DOWD, B.A.

The answering in general was poor. The working out of the questions was very often inaccurate, and the students had not kept up the work of the previous year as well as they should have done. The new work of the Middle Grade had been fairly prepared.

JUNIOR GRADE.—BOYS.

Report of P. A. E. DOWLING, B.A., and ROV. P. KEOGHAN, B.A.

Taken as a whole the results of the examination on this subject can scarcely be considered satisfactory. The answering in many instances was of a very medium character, while more than 10 per cent. of the papers sent in were absolutely worthless, the examinees showing no knowledge whatsoever of the subject. It very often occurred that where the principles underlying a correct solution were understood the work was marred by gross blunders of calculation. These mistakes, when not the result of carelessness, were often traceable to a want of neatness and method in the work. Teachers should be careful to impress on their pupils the great necessity for neatness as it is mainly by it accuracy can be ensured. The absence of method was particularly observable in the questions treating of fractions and it was frequently impossible to follow the process by which the answer was obtained from the fragmentary way in which the work was done. We think it well to observe that in dealing with complex fractions the various portions of the question should not be simplified piecemeal, but after transferring the question on to the answer book its several parts should be simplified concurrently, so that the examiner will see at a glance the entire work. Sufficient attention too had not been paid to the relative binding effects of the signs, nor to the use of brackets, which were fruitful sources of error. The two methods of treating fractions preparatory to the extraction of the square root, viz.:—(1) making the denominator a perfect square, or (2) reducing the fraction to a decimal, should be more carefully taught, as we only remember meeting five instances where the former and comparatively few where the latter method was adopted. While calling attention to these defects we gladly bear testimony to the excellent work sent in by several candidates.

JUNIOR GRADE.—GIRLS.

Report of Rev. JAMES DOWD, B.A.

The average of answering was fair. The students were not always able to recognise questions put in an unusual or new form. Inaccuracies in working out questions were far too common.

JUNIOR GRADE.—BOYS—OVER-AGE.

Report of Rev. JAMES DOWD, B.A.

The answering was very varied, in some cases remarkably good, in some cases bad. The general average was not what it should be.

PREPARATORY GRADE.—BOYS.

Report of P. A. E. DOWLING, B.A., and F. A. WHITTON.

The answering on the whole was highly satisfactory, the failures being but a very small proportion of the entire number examined, while of those who passed the great majority obtained high honour marks. In the main, the candidates were thoroughly well prepared and exhibited a good general knowledge of the subject. As usual, questions requiring the exercise of the reflective faculties were those in which the students were least successful. It is right to add that the execution of the work, in most instances, showed care and neatness.

PREPARATORY GRADE.—GIRLS.

Report of Rev. JAMES DOWD, B.A.

The answering was in general very good, and in very many cases excellent. If this is kept up the answering of these students in the Junior and Middle Grades when they come to these grades ought to exhibit a decided advance on that for the present year in both grades.

BOOK-KEEPING.

MIDDLE GRADE.—BOYS AND GIRLS.

Report of F. A. WHITTON.

Of the boys examined on this occasion less than one twelfth failed.

Of those who passed, honour marks were obtained by a smaller proportion than in the preceding year. I attribute this to the fact that while the candidates exhibited a good general knowledge of the elementary portion of the subject, they were somewhat deficient in the more advanced part requiring some exercise of thought and consideration.

With respect to girls, less than one-fourth failed.

In the case of both boys and girls, I am glad to be able again to state that, in most cases, the penmanship and execution of the work were highly creditable.

JUNIOR GRADE.—BOYS AND GIRLS.

Report of F. A. WHITTON.

Although the number of boys examined is largely in excess of that in the preceding year the proportion of those who failed, slightly over one-fourth, is nearly identical. Out of those who passed, however, a larger proportion obtained honour marks on this occasion.

In the case of girls the candidates were nearly double those in 1895. In the present year the proportion of failures was considerably less than one-fourth, and of those who passed more than one-half obtained honours.

I am of opinion that the students who passed were generally **well** prepared, and possessed a good practical knowledge of the subject.

The execution of the work as regards handwriting and formation of figures was, on the whole, very good.

NATURAL PHILOSOPHY.

JUNIOR, MIDDLE, AND SENIOR GRADES.— BOYS AND GIRLS.

Report of GEORGE COFFEY, B.E., and J. JOLY, D.Sc., F.R.S.

In the Junior Grade the answering is on the whole indicative of careful preparation. The number of passes is high, and among the candidates obtaining honours there are many of much merit both as regards the degree of understanding displayed and the style in which the questions have been answered.

There is one feature, however, in the manner in which the students are prepared for this examination which is not a matter of congratulation and which is conspicuously revealed in the answers to some of the questions upon the paper. The preparation appears to be, in an undue degree, of the nature of "grinding" and the knowledge displayed by the students, in the large majority of cases, shows a serious lack of practical teaching by experiments.

The powers of observation of the student seem to be, in fact, left uncultivated. He cannot distinguish or describe any difference in the physical properties of common substances, such as iron, water, sand and air, while he can answer with perfect facility a question on the velocity acquired by a body falling at the surface of the moon. A large number of those attempting the question upon the physical properties offer a string of scholastic definitions often *completely misapplied*, as "porosity, extensibility, elasticity, penetrability," etc., etc. This, in our opinion, reveals a most serious deficiency in the preparation. It strikes the examiner at once that a pupil who cannot answer this question is very unlikely to understand the meaning of "*g*" or appreciate, outside mere definition, any distinction between mass, inertia, and weight. Many indeed answer questions on the latter with perfect precision, quoting certain classical definitions, who cannot say in what respects water and iron differ from one another. Again, many attempting the question on specific gravity quote the formula correctly while representing in the diagram the most impossible modes of carrying out the experiment.

All this points to the conclusion that too much is attempted in this Junior course, and too little taught as it should be taught. The one aim in teaching Physics should be to give the pupil an intelligent interest in the natural phenomena around him. A book-knowledge of definitions and formulæ, not verified and explained to the student by reference to nature, is not of much value. In short, the idea derived from a perusal of the majority of the answers is that while the preparation has been most careful it is not of the right sort; rather tending to narrow and cripple the understanding, by transcending its capabilities and ignoring its functions, than to lead it out to a contemplation of the phenomena of nature. Until experimental teaching and experimental learning are introduced into schools generally this evil has little chance of being abolished.

It is quite to be expected from the existence of the evil alluded to that the answering in the higher grades should show but little advance over the merit displayed in the Junior Grade. In the Senior and Middle Grades neither the style nor matter of the answers have improved above those displayed by the younger candidates in a degree corresponding to the difference of age. Quite easy questions involving a little knowledge of what is measurable by experimental means are attempted by the most impossible suggestions. This would be at once remedied by experimental teaching; when, even if the student's memory failed him as to the correct procedure, he would not hazard such a suggestion as that of measuring the velocity of sound in a rod six feet long by stationing an observer at each end with watches, who are to observe the interval elapsing between sending and receiving a signal through the rod. Again, in the Middle Grade, whereas the numerical questions were constantly answered correctly, very few, even approximately, correct answers were given to a simple question on the pressure of a vapour in presence of its liquid.

There were in these grades, however, many cases to which the above criticism does not apply, but in which the student really appeared to appreciate the principles of the science and the possibilities of physical measurement.

CHEMISTRY.

JUNIOR, MIDDLE, AND SENIOR GRADES.—(BOYS AND GIRLS).

Report of E. A. LETTS, PH.D., F.C.S.

With reference to this year's examinations in Chemistry I beg to report as follows :—

On the whole the answering was good, and showed that the boys and girls had been carefully prepared. But I must again draw attention to the nearly complete ignorance shown by nearly all the candidates in the Middle and Senior Grades of practical work. The only remedy I can suggest is, that future examiners should be instructed to set more questions in this subject or to put a higher value on them.

DRAWING.

OBJECT DRAWING.

SENIOR GRADE.—BOYS AND GIRLS.

Report of JOHN CARROLL.

The result of the examination in this subject is good, only 14 papers out of a total of 57 having failed to obtain 25 per cent. of the maximum number of marks, while 23 papers secured 50 per cent. or more.

The faults to be noted in examining the drawings are (1) excessive darkness of the shadows, (2) exaggerated effects of reflected light, and (3) misapplication of the elementary principles of perspective, i.e., representing the objects rather as they are, than as they appear under the conditions given on the examination paper. For instance, some candidates have made drawings of the open book, showing all the four corners as right angles, and all the edges of their actual length. It is obviously impossible for the book, lying flat upon a table of the ordinary height, to have that appearance, unless the eyes of the candidates were placed immediately over the centre of the book.

PERSPECTIVE AND PROJECTION OF SHADOWS, ETC.

SENIOR GRADE.—BOYS AND GIRLS.

Report of W. E. CROWTHER.

There was a fair proportion of satisfactory papers containing really conscientious work, but in question 4 the pyramid was in all cases drawn with its most distant edge only parallel to the picture, instead of the whole of the most distant face being so placed. Owing to this no candidate quite obtained full marks.

It is regrettable that no attempt is made to teach this subject by the more direct and practical method which avoids the use of measuring points, and which is now employed in most examinations.

In the Projection of Shadows section, many failed in the preliminary projection of the solids, and the work in this subject was not at all equal to that in Perspective, which appears to be the more attractive subject.

FREEHAND.

MIDDLE GRADE.—BOYS.

Report of JOHN CARROLL.

Of the 241 papers entrusted to me for examination in this Grade, about three-fifths secured at least 25 per cent. of the total number of marks given for this subject, and of these over 100 papers obtained 50 per cent. at least. One or two exercises secured full marks, and several others came very near the maximum.

It may be interesting and instructive to both teachers and pupils to point out what qualities in the drawing of the example are necessary to secure a high percentage of marks. They are (1) Proportion, (2) Balance or Symmetry, (3) Continuity of line, or the connection between the several visible parts of the two leading lines or stems of the foliated ornament.

Most of the marks have been lost through not seeing, or, at any rate, not representing this feature—the skeleton or frame-work of the design on which all the rest either hangs or is built up.

MIDDLE GRADE.—GIRLS.

Report of EDWARD S. O'BRIEN, R.E.

Much excellent work was done in this subject, some 64 per cent. of the candidates having obtained marks varying from 100 to 200, 4 per cent. from 200 to 250, and but 2 per cent. showed practically entire want of knowledge by only obtaining from 0 to 25.

Students would do well to see that their pencils, &c., are suitable and in proper order, as some otherwise capital drawings were spoilt by coarse and rough outlines.

That the example, though by no means easy, was one eminently suitable is shown by the results and it is most creditable to both students and teachers that so few unprepared candidates presented themselves for examination and that so many obtained high marks.

PRACTICAL GEOMETRY.

MIDDLE GRADE.—BOYS AND GIRLS.

Report of W. E. CROWTHER.

The discrepancy between the gross number of marks obtainable and the number actually awarded in this examination is so great as to suggest that no adequate attempt is made to realize the requirements of the programme, and a very cursory inspection of the papers is sufficient to show that a large proportion of the candidates have entered the examination without hope of success.

No other conclusion than this is possible when so many blank sheets, so many sheets without examination numbers, and so many sheets bearing other evidence of carelessness, are sent in. Thus one-half of the candidates apparently did not take the trouble to bring scales, squares, &c.,

or to use them, and although the girls' papers indicate greater readiness of application than the boys', many of the answers are merely misapplied reminiscences of text-book diagrams, betraying inability to deal with the smallest deviations from stock problems such as require efforts of the reasoning or imaginative powers.

FREEHAND.

JUNIOR GRADE.—BOYS.

Report of JOHN CARROLL.

The results of the examination in Freehand drawing of the Junior Grade boys is decidedly good, over 70 per cent. of the exercises having secured at least 25 per cent. of the maximum number of marks whilst, of these, considerably more than half have gained 50 per cent. or over.

In examining the drawings of this grade, the two most important features that have to be considered are (1) Proportion, and (2) Balance or Symmetry.

In cases where either of these have been ignored very few, if any, marks have been awarded.

I regret to state that there are still some papers that indicate ignorance of even the simplest and most obvious mode of construction for a symmetrical figure viz. that of drawing a centre line first on which to build up and balance the copy of the example.

JUNIOR GRADE.—GIRLS.

Report of W. E. CROWTHER.

The marks awarded are a sufficient attestation of the general excellence of this year's work.

As is usual in copying vase forms there is some weakness in regard to balance. If the simple expedient of reversal or inversion were more resorted to the fault would be overcome. Want of success in grasping the general shape or proportions of the object was also apparent, suggesting that students should acquire the habit of viewing the example and copy from a distance, as by holding the paper at arms length occasionally. Any device which thus give a new view of the work cannot be too highly estimated as a means of freshening the judgment.

JUNIOR GRADE.—BOYS.—OVER-AGE.

Report of EDWARD S. O'BRIEN, B.E.

That much of the work done in this subject was good is shown by the fact that about 52 per cent. obtained from 100 to 200 marks and 9 per cent. 200 to 250.

But on the other hand 9 per cent. of the candidates obtained marks varying from 0 to 25, which, in Freehand drawing, may be taken as indicating entire absence of preparation in such candidates, as a student could hardly fail to obtain over 25 marks even though wanting in natural aptitude, had he received any teaching on the subject.

Some candidates have done their drawings the same size as the examples and of these a few possibly from want of attention to the directions printed on the examination papers.

PRACTICAL GEOMETRY.

JUNIOR GRADE.—BOYS.

Report of W. R. CROWTHER and EDWARD S. O'BRIEN, B.E.

A gratifying degree of excellence is manifest in the work of this examination, 86 per cent. of the candidates having obtained marks varying from 100 to 200. There was much evidence of good and careful teaching. The fact that over 5 per cent. secured no marks at all appears to show, however, considerable laxity in regard to the presentation of quite unprepared students.

We have also to note that there is much want of clearness as to methods, and that many candidates have lost marks by neglect of the rule requiring that all construction lines shall be clearly shown.

Greater attention should be given to neatness of working, the possession and proper employment of scales, set squares and other instruments. Scarcely any candidates attempted to rule in properly the sectional shading of question 7.

In the plan of the hexagonal pyramid the diagonals were commonly omitted, apparently by inadvertence. It was rare to find a satisfactorily constructed ellipse, and many attempts were made to gain a proportion of marks by sketchy suggestions of construction, not fair either to other candidates or to the examiners.

The very simple construction necessary for three circles in contact was not generally known, and few candidates realised that a scale of one-thirtieth is two-fifths of an inch to the foot.

JUNIOR GRADE.—GIRLS.

Report of ALICE M. KEOGH.

In this subject the answers ranked themselves, generally speaking, into either of two classes : good and bad. Some of the papers done by candidates were most excellent, the problems well and neatly worked, and Geometry evidently well understood; other papers showed great carelessness, and the work was rough and clumsy.

Many of the candidates made little or even no attempt to answer the questions.

Question No. 5 was omitted by many, and many others gave an answer on scales that had little merit in itself and had no reference to the question.

Question No. 3 appears to have been more frequently answered by guesswork than by any knowledge of the problem.

Some of the answer sheets had the work done on both sides, which is most inconvenient for the examiner as sometimes the work on the second side escapes notice in the first instance.

FREEHAND.

PREPARATORY GRADE.—BOYS.

Report of ALICE M. KEOGH[1]

On the whole the drawings were fair and well placed upon the paper. Some of the drawings were so excellent that they obtained, in some cases full, in others almost full, marks ; but on the other hand, there were a number of very poor drawings.

Many of the candidates who went in for the examination were evidently not qualified for it, either from want of sufficient instruction or some other cause.

The majority of the candidates missed the *character* of the object.

Many, in their desire to make a *good line* or a *neat* drawing, overlooked the more essential qualities of the *character* of the object, and *proportion*.

PREPARATORY GRADE.—GIRLS.

Report of EDWARD S. O'BRIEN, B.A.

Much excellence was shown by the candidates in this grade, no less than 53 per cent. obtaining from 100 to 200 marks, and nearly 10 per cent. from 200 to 300, while the number making little or no attempt at work was very small.

Students would do well to pay more attention to the correctness of their outlines, as nearly all lost more or less marks through their drawings being distorted, many of the best finished failing badly in this respect.

Candidates should also take more care to provide themselves with suitable drawing materials, without which clear and neat outlines cannot be obtained.

On the whole the examination may be considered to reflect credit on both the candidates and their teachers.

SHORTHAND.

JUNIOR, MIDDLE, and SENIOR GRADES.—BOYS and GIRLS.

Report of HENRY HOLT and CHARLES RYAN.

We are glad to be able to report an improvement in the answering this year in all the grades. We believe this has been to a considerable extent due to our action last year, when we were compelled to reject a large number of candidates who had entered without sufficient preparation. Such want of preparation was not apparent this year, for those who presented themselves were, as a rule, much better grounded in the system. In no respect was the improvement more remarkable than in the answering on the "B" paper (translation from Shorthand into Longhand). Many of the candidates in 1893, especially in the Junior and Middle Grades, showed a gross ignorance of spelling; and in the "A" paper a large number were unacquainted with even the elementary principles of phonography. This year, the work on the "B" paper was creditably done in many cases; and although in the "A" paper the improvement was not so great, there was an advance as compared with 1893 in all the grades.

We have, however, to notice that some candidates seem to think that the quantity of work done within the time allotted for the examination is of more importance than its quality; and that by hurriedly getting through the whole, or a large proportion of the papers, they can atone for careless and incorrect writing. Others, especially in the Junior Grade, while displaying an acquaintance with the most advanced abbreviating devices, which can be profitably used only by experienced writers of the system, manifested an ignorance of those elementary principles which should be thoroughly mastered in the first instance. A candidate who habitually confuses the characters for "l" and "sh," "m" and "n," "p" and "ch," or the "f" and "n" hooks, who writes "chart" instead of "part," "seem" for "soon," or "grove" instead of "grown," can never attain proficiency by adopting abbreviating principles suitable for the reporting style, but for the use of which he is utterly unfitted. Such students, if they are ever to become expert shorthand writers, should recommence at the beginning, and ground themselves carefully in the first principles. We have always awarded a larger number of marks to candidates who have done a substantial portion of the papers correctly and neatly, than to those who have attempted to write the entire hurriedly and incorrectly.

The experience gained from the examinations of 1893 led us to recommend the withdrawal this year of the "C" papers, containing questions on the theory, as we found that these papers gave an undue advantage to candidates who possessed a more theoretical knowledge, to the detriment of those who had acquired a more practical mastery of the system; and that many students, who were able to answer a large number of such questions, showed, by their unsatisfactory work on the practical "A" and "B" papers, that they were incapable of applying the rules, which they had evidently learned by rote, without understanding their meaning or application. The result of this year's examination confirms us in the view that the "C" papers supply no additional criterion of the candidates' knowledge of the system, which is better tested by the practical application of the rules required in working the "A" and "B" papers.

Exception was taken in some quarters to the length of the papers set in 1893. As a result of our experience of last year's examinations, we thought it better to reduce the number of words set in each grade, while still, however, requiring from every candidate a satisfactory knowledge of the system in order to qualify for passing.

MUSIC.

JUNIOR, MIDDLE, AND SENIOR GRADES.—(GIRLS ONLY).

Report of THOMAS GICK, MUS.D.

I beg to submit the following report on the examination of answer-books in the Theory of Music:

JUNIOR GRADE.

In NOTATION, SCALES, and INTERVALS the answering was generally good. Many of the students, however, lost time in writing out *all* the modes of the minor scale, instead of confining themselves to the mode asked for.

The answering in HARMONY was weak, particularly in figured Bass; only nine of the students succeeded in getting full marks.

The GENERAL RESULT is, however, very creditable to the Junior Grade, as of the 628 students 235 passed, 213 passed with honours, and of this latter number no less than 18 scored marks numbering from 400 to 475. 180 failed in obtaining the requisite number for a pass.

MIDDLE GRADE.

SCALES.—The answering was fairly good; but marks were lost by some students writing their answer in a mode which is practically obsolete, and would not be likely to be met with in any of their vocal or instrumental music.

KEY RELATIONSHIP.—The answering in this part of the subject was not good, the majority having but a misty idea of the relationship of keys.

HARMONY.—The answering to questions 4 and 7 was generally weak, and in the Figured Bass exercise—No. 10—only one succeeded in obtaining full marks.

HISTORY.—In this also the answering was not satisfactory by many of the students, only one obtaining full marks.

TRANSPOSITION.—The exercise was well done by a large majority of the students. Of the 182 examined 79 passed, 55 passed with honours, and 58 failed to obtain the requisite number for a pass.

SENIOR GRADE.—Seventy examined.

INTERVALS AND SCALES.—The answering was fairly good.

ACCENT.—Not so good.

MUSICAL FORM.—On this question only two got full marks, many of the students making no distinction between the Concerto and Sonata forms of composition.

MUSICAL HISTORY.—The answering was generally good.

TRANSPOSITION was also good, students showing an intelligent acquaintance with the scales connected with the transposition of the exercise.

FIGURED BASS.—The answering was good. Students, however, would find their difficulties lessened if they gave themselves more space when adding the figured harmonies.

COUNTERPOINT TO A GIVEN SUBJECT.—This was fairly well done, but none of the students answered sufficiently well to entitle them to full marks. In this exercise there was a sequential progression which should have been sequentially harmonised. Evidently none observed this, otherwise their work would have been better and presented fewer difficulties.

RESULT.—32 passed, 27 passed with honours, and 11 failed to obtain the requisite number for a pass.

GENERAL OBSERVATIONS.

Comparing the answering of the examination just held to that of 1885, when I last examined, there is a decided improvement in the general knowledge displayed by nearly all the students in the Theory of Music. In assigning the marks to the several questions—within the rules fixed by the Commissioners—I assigned the largest number to those questions which required the longest study and widest knowledge to their successful answering.

I observed, particularly in the Junior Grade, that many students did not place their examination number on the music paper. This should be done as well as on the answer book; for, if by any chance the music sheet got separated from the answer book on which the number is placed, there would be little, if anything, to identify it with the answer book.

BOTANY.

Junior, Middle, and Senior Grades.—Girls only.

Report of George Sigerson, m.d.

I have the honour to report that I have examined the papers of 101 candidates in the Junior Grade, of 47 candidates in the Middle Grade, and of 9 candidates in the Senior Grade.

Notwithstanding a certain percentage of failures, the papers in all the Grades appear on the whole to indicate honest work, and bear evidence to the intelligent industry of the candidates. There are some papers, indeed, which deserve high commendation, and exhibit proof of exact study and scientific teaching.

I noted last year that the Senior Grade did not seem to carry out the promise shown in the work of the Middle Grade. With fuller opportunity for forming an opinion in this, my second year, I find the facts confirm that view. The candidates in the Senior Grade have, indeed, done well, but their number falls below what it should be, if the members of the Middle Grade of last year had been drafted into it.

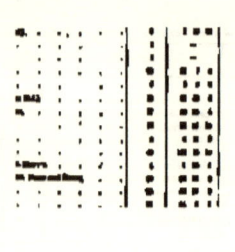

List of Parishes in the Districts of which Births were Paid in 1894, and Amounts of such Fees—continued.

County	Union	Place of Service	No. of Midwife paid Fees	Fees, amount paid	Auditor's fees (under Vaccination Acts)	Expenses over and above ordinary payments
		Brought forward	100	105	1	[illegible]
[illegible]	[illegible]	[illegible]	5	6	[illegible]	[illegible]
	[illegible]	[illegible]	5	5	[illegible]	[illegible]
[illegible]	[illegible]	[illegible]	8	8	[illegible]	[illegible]
	[illegible]	[illegible]	8	8	[illegible]	[illegible]
	[illegible]	[illegible]	7	9	[illegible]	[illegible]
	[illegible]	[illegible]	8	8	[illegible]	[illegible]
[illegible]	[illegible]	[illegible]	56	59	[illegible]	[illegible]
[illegible]	[illegible]	[illegible]	8	9	[illegible]	[illegible]
[illegible]	[illegible]	[illegible]	8	9	[illegible]	[illegible]
[illegible]	[illegible]	[illegible]	7	8	[illegible]	[illegible]
[illegible]	[illegible]	[illegible]	30	32	[illegible]	[illegible]
[illegible]	[illegible]	[illegible]	46	49	[illegible]	[illegible]
[illegible]	[illegible]	[illegible]	8	9	[illegible]	[illegible]
	[illegible]	[illegible]	80	84	[illegible]	[illegible]
	[illegible]	[illegible]	8	9	[illegible]	[illegible]
[illegible]	[illegible]	[illegible]	31	33	[illegible]	[illegible]
		TOTAL	459	497	[illegible]	[illegible]

APPENDIX V.

THE BURKE MEMORIAL PRIZES.

A sum of money, subscribed in memory of the late THOMAS HENRY BURKE, Esq., Under Secretary to the Lord Lieutenant, was transferred by the Burke Memorial Committee, on 18th March, 1884, to the Intermediate Education Board for Ireland, who undertook to administer the Fund in accordance with the following Rules—(the sum funded is £1,222 18s. 11d. Consols):—

I. The annual income from the fund shall be applied in paying three Prizes, one of £15, one of £10, and a second of £10; any surplus or deficiency to be apportioned in the same ratio. If, in the opinion of the Commissioners, sufficient merit be not shown by the Candidates competing to justify the award of any or either of the Prizes, the amount of such Prize may be, at the discretion of the Board, withheld and added to the principal.

II. No student shall be qualified to receive these Prizes except the children of persons who are or have been, in receipt of salary or pension in Ireland, paid out of money derived from Parliamentary Grants, Rates or Taxes, other than members of the Naval or Military Services, not being also in Civil employment.

III. The Prizes shall be awarded as follows:—that of £15 to the Boy whom, at the annual Examination in the Junior Grade among Male Candidates qualified in the manner expressed in the next preceding Rule, the Board shall adjudge to rank highest in answering; One Prize of £10 to the Boy whom in the same Grade at such Examination the Board shall adjudge to rank second among such persons in answering; and the other of £10 to the Girl whom, at such Examination in the same Grade, among Female Candidates qualified in the manner aforesaid, the Board shall adjudge to rank highest in answering.

IV. The decision of the Board shall be final and decisive in determining whether the Candidates fulfil the conditions of the third Rule.

V. The Board may deduct all expenses connected with the trust from the yearly income.

No. 4944.

Dublin Castle,
16th March, 1895.

GENTLEMEN,

I have to acknowledge the receipt of your letter of the 15th instant, forwarding, for submission to His Excellency the Lord Lieutenant, the Annual Report of the Intermediate Education Board for Ireland for the year 1894.

I am,
Gentlemen,
Your obedient Servant,

(Signed)   D. HARREL.

The Assistant Commissioners
of Intermediate Education,
1, Hume-street

Dublin: Printed for Her Majesty's Stationery Office,
By Alex. Thom & Co. (Limited), 87, 88, & 89, Abbey-street,
The Queen's Printing Office.